NEW YORK REVIEW BOOKS
CLASSICS

THE SILENTIARY

ANTONIO DI BENEDETTO (1922–1986) was born in
Mendoza, Argentina. He began his career as a journalist, writing
for the Mendoza paper *Los Andes*. In 1953 he published his first
book, a collection of short stories titled *Mundo animal*. *Zama*
(published as an NYRB Classic) was his first novel; it was
followed by *El silenciero*, *Los suicidas*, and *Sombras, nada más...*
Over the course of his career he received numerous honors,
including a 1975 Guggenheim Fellowship and decorations from
the French and Italian governments, and he earned the admiration
of the likes of Jorge Luis Borges, Julio Cortázar, and Roberto
Bolaño. In 1976, Di Benedetto was imprisoned and tortured by
Argentina's military dictatorship; after his release in 1977 he
went into exile in Spain. He returned to Buenos Aires in 1984,
where he died less than two years later.

ESTHER ALLEN received the 2017 National Translation
Award for her translation of Antonio Di Benedetto's *Zama*.
A cofounder of the PEN World Voices Festival in New York
City, she teaches at the City University of New York Graduate
Center and Baruch College, where she directs the Sidney
Harman Writer-in-Residence Program.

JUAN JOSÉ SAER (1937–2005) was an Argentine novelist who
settled in France in 1968, where he taught literature at the
University of Rennes for many years. His books include *The
Witness*, *Nobody Nothing Never*, *The Event*, and *The Investigation*.

THE SILENTIARY

ANTONIO DI BENEDETTO

Translated from the Spanish by
ESTHER ALLEN

Introduction by
JUAN JOSÉ SAER

NEW YORK REVIEW BOOKS

New York

THIS IS A NEW YORK REVIEW BOOK
PUBLISHED BY THE NEW YORK REVIEW OF BOOKS
435 Hudson Street, New York, NY 10014
www.nyrb.com

This work is published with the support of the Sur Translation Support Program
run by Argentina's Ministry of Foreign Affairs, International Commerce, and
Worship.
*Obra editada en el marco del Programa "Sur" de Apoyo a las Traducciones del
Ministerio de Relaciones Exteriores y Culto de la República Argentina*

The translation of this novel was supported by a 2018 Guggenheim Fellowship.
Antonio Di Benedetto was also the recipient of a Guggenheim Fellowship
in 1973. The Guggenheim Foundation's generous assistance is gratefully
acknowledged by the translator.

The excerpt from Arthur Schopenhauer's "On Noise" is adapted from the translation by T. Bailey Saunders in *Studies in Pessimism*.

First published as a New York Review Book Classic in 2022.

Library of Congress Cataloging-in-Publication Data
Names: Di Benedetto, Antonio, 1922–1986, author. | Allen, Esther, 1962–
    translator. | Saer, Juan José, 1937–2005, writer of introduction.
Title: The silentiary / by Antonio di Benedetto; translated by Esther Allen;
    introduction by Juan José Saer.
Other titles: Silenciero. English
Description: New York: New York Review Books, [2022] | Series: New York
    Review Books classics
Identifiers: LCCN 2021012496 | ISBN 9781681375625 (paperback) |
    ISBN 9781681375632 (ebook)
Classification: LCC PQ7797.B4343 S513 2021 | DDC 863/.64—dc23
LC record available at https://lccn.loc.gov/2021012496

ISBN 978-1-68137-562-5
Available as an electronic book; ISBN 978-1-68137-563-2

Printed in the United States of America on acid-free paper.
10 9 8 7 6 5 4 3 2 1

CONTENTS

INTRODUCTION

IN THE unity of style and subject matter that governs them, Antonio Di Benedetto's principal novels, *Zama*, *The Silentiary*, and *The Suicides*, comprise a kind of trilogy and, let it be stated once and for all, constitute one of the culminating moments of twentieth-century narrative fiction in Spanish. Di Benedetto is one of the few writers in Argentine literature to have devised a style entirely his own, grounded in frugality and precision. For all its terseness and apparent poverty, however, this style is highly nuanced, by turns colloquial or philosophical, descriptive or lyrical. Its power is astonishing. Equally startling is Di Benedetto's technical skill—an expression that wouldn't have pleased him and that doesn't entirely convince me—which his discretion, a personal trait that is rare in our time, always leaves in the background. Every story's events are organized by its internal tensions, and Di Benedetto masterfully distills those events, assigning each one its precise place within the whole. Caprice plays no role in the construction of his novels. With a sure and skillful hand, his subtle artistry discards all superfluous rhetoric to concentrate on the essential.

Of this singular art, *The Silentiary* is one of the summits. First published in 1964, the novel carries forward the soliloquy launched in *Zama* in 1956 and later continued in *The Suicides* (1966). Read together, the three works form a tacit system that aims to represent the world, whose noise, in *The Silentiary*, is simply a metonymic variant, yet another "instrument of not-allowing-to-be." From Don Diego de Zama's comic abandonment to the methodical inventory of the causes and circumstances that can legitimize suicide, man, in Di Benedetto's work, is trapped by the destructive noise of the world. And the silentiary—an admirable neologism that displays both Di Benedetto's conceptual precision and his fine ear for the elusive evocations of speech—a nameless personage locked within his persecuting universe, who only succeeds in making his torture eternal when he resolves to neutralize its causes, stands out, even among the many memorable figures that emerge against the unmistakable landscape of Di Benedetto's fiction.

Those who would derive the novel from the epic, no doubt with good historical reason, must henceforth abandon their cause in defeat: this unusual trilogy has no use for the epic's moralizing, its melodramatic scrap heaps of gold and silver. Di Benedetto's characters struggle (in silence, we might say), riveted to the impossibility of living, like live insects pinned to a naturalist's chart by the sharp and wounding point of some obsession: an unreasonable hope, suicide, or the noises that "act upon your being." The ingenuity Adorno finds in the epic, the immersion in concrete reality, the pure action freed from the paralyzing venom of reflexive consciousness, only exists as legend among Di Benedetto's characters: Zama's or Besarión's "departure," or the writing that promises finally to bestow plenitude and thereby emancipation from the servitude imposed by the external world on the narrator of *The Silentiary*, who confesses, "By day, I thought that even in my dreams I lacked all talent or ambition for heroism."

The consciousness of this nameless narrator, at once omnipresent and discreet, diagrams a succession of events until it reaches a point where perception and delirium, common sense and paranoid rationalization, become—without emphasis or explanation, be it psychological or of any other sort—a piercing image of the world's painful complexity. The question of whether the anomaly dwells within our consciousness or in things themselves turns out to be insignificant, of no use whatsoever in solving the problem. World and consciousness, joined in secret but constant struggle, tumble together to their perdition. We can, of course, believe it is the unforeseeable breath of dementia that blows here on the hot coals of obsession, but the final silent protest also seems legitimate and sincere: "'Martyr for having aspired to live my own life, and not someone else's, not the life that is imposed,' my justification clamors within me."

The life that is imposed, that is: the inhuman weight of the external world. For the silentiary (the "maker of silence" or *hacedor de silencio*, as I once heard Di Benedetto himself say, pleased by a nuance the title acquired in one of its translations) the multiplicity of noise derives from its many sources, yes—and also from its many possible meanings.

Noise introduces accident into the world, asymmetry, suffering. For the narrator, that which precedes the creation of the world is darkness and silence, towards which everything tends back. "Our noisy years," as Shakespeare might say,* are merely an adverse parenthesis, a painful interruption of stasis, one particular case within the intolerable cycle of rebirths into the prison of appearances from which, according to

---

*Or as Wordsworth did say: "Our noisy years seem moments in the being / Of the eternal Silence: truths that wake, / To perish never...": William Wordsworth, "Ode: Intimations of Immortality from Recollections of Early Childhood" (1807).

Buddhist doctrine, only bodhi, "awakening," can liberate the saint into the definitive nonconsciousness of extinction. But, in its connotation of superficiality, noise also represents wordliness, and implies an irreflexive, almost programmatic social conduct, whether as a form of opposition, or as the hyperaffirmative postulation of oneself or even of a generational imperative. The expression "get in the noise," which the narrator defines as a slogan of the age, posits noise as the embodiment of all that is optimal, the positive essence of existence, and therefore the source of the universe's final justification. A war of principles thus exists between the narrator and the world, an organic antagonism, irreconcilable and extreme. Finally, another of the many aspects of noise's multiplicity, and perhaps the most destructive of them all, is that of the ambiguity of its origins and character, and of the true cause of its omnipresence. For it seems all too difficult to know with any certainty whether its enemy waves, lacerating but blind, reach into us from the outside, or whether they expand outward surreptitiously from some obscure place, an intimate source both internal and remote, deranging both us and the things of this world. The paradox reaches its apogee when, at a given moment in the struggle and sometimes perhaps from its very beginning, Di Benedetto's characters seem to change sides and ally themselves with the world, collaborating in their own defeat. In the final scene of *Zama*, the sublime "I might not die. Not yet," expresses less the hope of prolonging life—the body reduced to bloody stumps, consciousness to a faint, groggy dream—than the certainty of continuing to endure an endless parade of losses and humiliations. In this, and in their particular feeling for vileness, their own and that of others, Di Benedetto's characters have a distant affiliation with certain of Dostoyevsky's heroes. But their secret wounds, their isolation and irony, and especially the slightly masochistic irony in their view of themselves, makes them closer kin to the characters of Svevo, Pessoa, and Kafka.

Before concluding, I find it impossible not to address a central matter in Argentine literature: the narrative prose of Antonio Di Benedetto. His prose is undoubtedly the most original of the century. Useless to seek antecedents for his style, influences: he has none. Much like the Judeo-Christian cosmogony—that is, the world in which we live—Di Benedetto's style appears to have emerged from nothingness. In that respect, it is superior to our world, which required six days of its creator's time to be completed. From his first sentence, Di Benedetto's prose was fully developed, ready to perform. In Borges we occasionally find echoes of Hazlitt, Marcel Schwob, Oscar Wilde, or Macedonio Fernández; in Roberto Arlt, the Russian writers, Pirandello, the Futurists. But while certain themes in Di Benedetto's work have an affinity with those of existentialism—the ghosts of Kierkegaard, Schopenhauer, and Camus drift along the back of the stage from time to time—the prose that discreetly distributes them across the page has neither precursors nor successors. At a time when lengthy "poetical" sentences and strident emphases (impactful chapter endings, erotic or existential dithyrambs) were in vogue, Di Benedetto's aesthetic sobriety—far too enmeshed in the insidious morass of the real to be distracted by these rhetorical artifices, which did not suit his temperament—was ignored for decades by successive and interchangeable fabricators of reputations because it pursued a unique personal path of probity and lucidity. Though from the start a tiny group of readers, gradually increasing in number over the years, was able to recognize the obvious genius of his fiction, and though a few translations and reissued editions have come out in recent decades, the immense debt that Argentine culture owes to Antonio Di Benedetto has yet to be settled. The prizes he won, which he proudly listed on the flaps of his books, were ridiculously disproportionate to the texts they were meant to reward. We might almost say, when we consider the profound meaning of those texts, that those prizes merely attest to an anachronism. Well intentioned though they were, such local acknowledgements—municipal, provincial, or national; governmental or corporate—cast an equivocal light upon a body of work that is at once cerebral and gut-wrenching. In the subjects it addresses and the wise artistry of its composition, Di Benedetto's writing is of universal significance.

—JUAN JOSÉ SAER
Paris, 1999

THE SILENTIARY

If it had occurred, the story here postulated could have taken place in a city in Latin America as of the late postwar era (the years 1950 and thereafter are plausible).

I

THE FRONT gate gives onto the dingy tiled patio. I open the gate and meet the noise.

I look around for it, as if its shape and the extent of its vitality could be determined. It comes from beyond the bedrooms, from an empty lot I've never seen, behind a spacious house that faces a different street.

"It's been like this all morning," my mother warns from the kitchen threshold.

"What is it?" I want to establish, disconcerted.

"They brought a bus, turned on the engine, and left it running…"

I make no move to come in, so she lets me know: "Your uncle's here. He'll have lunch with us. He's reading the news."

On the dining room table, the sun pours its bounty upon the daily paper. Naming that bounty is part of the lunchtime ritual, as necessary as saying grace.

But we can't proceed as usual. The unending noise compels us to think of it, rather than anything else.

"How do you know it's a bus?"

"I asked your uncle to go have a look."

Her brother expends a small movement of the head in support of this statement.

The explanation for the errand is implicit: since the noise

began, she's been flustered and disturbed, worried on her son's account.

"It can't last. A bus comes and goes," my uncle opines.

The pressure of the noise in my head drives me to question this.

"'Comes and goes' is an expression. A bus comes and goes when it's driving down the street. But this bus is different, isn't it? It's been grafted onto our house. Can't you hear it? Of course, you won't have to endure it much longer, you don't live here..."

The spoon suspended in midair, soup overflowing—the only response offered by my uncle's surprise—dwarfs my vehemence and leaves me in wordless mortification.

A silence falls over the three of us. While it lasts, I enumerate the reasons for moderation he could give me. I'm venting my aggression and anger on him, thereby being boorishly unfair and blaming the wrong person. I've failed to account for the possibility that the noise will simply end once and for all and not come back. Instead, I stubbornly cling to the supposition that this problem has taken possession of the future and henceforth will grant us no respite. I've failed to keep in mind that the normal activity of a bus is to circulate here and there, always outside, and that to run the engine when the bus isn't moving is uneconomic and therefore must correspond to some sort of short-term test, nothing more.

To make amends for the blow, which also grazed my mother, I say, "All right, it will pass. Or we'll have recourse to the law, to make it pass."

Immediately I regret these words. It's as if I've now committed myself to an obscure battle for which I don't feel at all prepared: a welter of complaints, to whom I don't know, verifications, proofs, allegations, sanctions levied on others, the hostility of the still-unnamed guilty parties towards me.

The noise is interrupted by the second part of the workday I must put in at the office.

Later, back home, the front sidewalk marks the boundary of all my fears. Beyond it, the definitive conditions for battle may have been established.

Inside is only my mother, amid benign domestic sounds.

I don't ask how much longer the noise lasted. My mother says nothing to remind me of it, but her face and eyes are tired, and the way she serves me dinner betrays a haste to get to bed.

At dawn, the daylight a glaze of watery milk on the windowpanes, as my mind, jerked into a state of alertness, discerns a noise attached to the rear wall of my room, something like my heart grows agitated within me.

The impression of a motor lasts only a few minutes. After that, one by one, comes a sequence of operations that put the weighty vehicle into forward motion, then into reverse, then forward again, then reverse, and then finally enable it to thread its way through an exit. At that point it merges with the diffuse acoustics that accompany daybreak in every city and vanishes into the distance.

I'm relieved. "A bus comes and goes."

I wonder whether it also startled my mother awake and know that it did when she comes in—too early to pretend otherwise—with a good-morning smile and the painstaking breakfast she prepares for her bachelor son.

I won't call what's happening to us routine: a routine

numbs the senses, forms habits. This bus, every morning and every night, punctures our life with shocks.

Men's voices rise above the engine and its various maneuvers. Sometimes they convey the kind of words that are humiliating when we know a woman we respect is hearing them.

Though my mother and I say nothing to each other, these abrupt intrusions are making our lives wretched.

———

The doorbell.

"It's your friend ... Besarión."

My mother is somewhat resistant to Besarión, perhaps because he brings up questions to which she can find no answer.

"You say he never speaks to you at work. But here he does. Why?"

"He's a salesman, he's free, out on the street, while I'm at my desk. If he wanted to speak to me there, he could, of course. But he says I'm assistant manager of the unit and on track to be manager, but only manager in there, while he has the Power everywhere. And since he has the Power he can't be my subordinate simply because I work in an office."

"It's a bit complicated."

"Yes. True. A bit complicated."

"Anyway, he's subordinate to the other managers and assistant managers, isn't he?"

"Yes, but he says his dealings with me are on an intellectual plane, or sometimes he says spiritual."

"What is his power?"

I offer my mother a smile, begging her indulgence for my circuitous friend: I don't know what power he has either.

My mother doesn't know why my friendship with Besarión remains so external, why I never open the intimacy of our home to him.

It's because he's happy with conversation alone and doesn't demand conventional hospitality. And it's also because our contentious exchanges hide from prying eyes the fact that I, a grown man of twenty-five, lounge around in the doorway or on the sidewalk in a state of vigilant eagerness, or in the gratified tenderness of seeing her, whenever a visit from Besarión happens to coincide with Leila's emergence into the sunlight.

Besarión, too, is unaware of the purpose his lecturing serves for me.

"It's your friend ... Besarión."

In tones that admit of no dispute, Besarión demands I come and see something. I say I'll come, then ask where. But I've already consented.

"Should I change clothes?"

"No. We're going to my house."

"I have to be at the office at three. You won't make me late?"

"Before we go any farther, let's get things straight. Are you a boss or a clerk?"

Besarión is someone who charges into any fray. He often annoys me, but he's also sincere, good-hearted, and more ingenuous than cunning. I can forgive him, even jab at him a little.

"Let's get things straight. First: I'm not a clerk. I'm second-in-command after the boss. Second: I'm not the boss. I'm second-in-command after the boss."

We go on walking. Before leaving the block, I cast a glance over at where she might be, and isn't. Leila.

Besarión says, "I want to share the extent of human impurity with you."

He corrects himself. "The impurity of a man."

Midstatement he corrects course again. "Of a man and a woman."

I'm used to these inconsistencies, experienced in his mental gymnastics. They've trained me to reply, "Why limit it? If this particular man, this particular woman, has committed a vile action, then even if the act corresponds only to the negative aspects of the individual, in some way it represents the whole individual. You can state quite correctly: this act demonstrates the extent of human impurity."

"That's not my way. I don't generalize. To protect myself."

"How's that?"

"If H does something bad and thus I conclude that all men are bad, I thereby authorize H to deduce from a bad action by A that all men are bad. In the first case, I'm safe because I'm the one judging: I exclude myself and generalize to include everybody else. In the second case, no: because someone else is judging and generalizing, and he doesn't have to exclude me."

Besarión shares a table with his mother that is rarely set for more than two. His family life reiterates certain nuances, perhaps even certain essences, of my own. I'd already had hints of this; his story strengthens them. And establishes a difference: Besarión has sisters—from the same mother and father—but they are not in harmony with him and his mother, and have gone their separate ways. Their husbands are in business and prosper.

Besarión shows and explains. With his mother, he lives

in the apartment at the end of the hallway. The door just before theirs belongs to the building's owners. A small, precarious pipe, which may be the drain for the kitchen or laundry room, emerges near that penultimate doorway and spews a trail of dirty water towards the final door.

"It's deliberate," Besarión informs me, and I see that the flow of water is encouraged by the floor's uneven slope (towards the inside).

"Why are they doing this?"

"To get rid of us."

"But doesn't it bother them too?"

"They say some work's being done, that it's only for a few days."

We go inside.

With a broom, Besarión's mother is guiding the waters towards the drain in the courtyard. When she sees me—or upon being seen—she feels ashamed, weeps. She asks if I'm an engineer and says if her husband were alive this would soon be resolved.

My friend registers this remark, which diminishes him. As we walk through, he blurts, "I need a defense of some kind, otherwise this gets resolved the way my father would have done it."

He exhibits his hands, full of rage, and makes a resting fly his pretext for punching the wall. But misses.

He proffers a needless clarification: "I can't share the world with flies, alive or dead."

Then, after a steadying silence has elapsed: "I need legal counsel."

"I don't believe so. Just file a complaint."

"Perhaps. But I must not go to the Law through the Police. If a man of the Law situates me within the Law, by his side, and instructs me to do so, then I'll be prepared to enter a police station. Otherwise, no."

"I think you're complicating things."

"It is the Order of things. I cannot overturn Order."

"Then come to an understanding with a man of the Law, who will set you in 'Order.'"

"That's you."

"Me...? No."

"You went to law school."

"For a time. I don't have a degree and I've forgotten all of it." I compromise: "Some of my friends graduated. I can put you in touch with them."

He won't compromise.

I instruct him in a different sort of order. "You don't need a lawyer, you need a carpenter."

"You have an idea?"

"Yes."

Too much light comes in between the bottom edge of Besarión's front door and the hallway floor. He should have someone attach wooden slats there to seal it off tightly, so nothing can come through.

"I don't need a carpenter. I'll know how to do it—or I hope I will."

He tells me he inherited the tools of a trade and a craft. He was never trained and has never put the tools to use. Even so, he's in the habit of picking up clean, polished pieces of wood off the street. Others ignore them because they're too small, but he likes them.

"They'll be useful," he says, "to contain the impurity."

He's glad.

He takes leave of me.

*

It's morning and I'm at the office. Someone brings me a piece of paper, from Besarión: "I closed it off with wood and sealed it with a rag. I slept well. When I opened the door, there was water up to my knees. It washed inside and now the whole house is filthy. Because the door was sealed, the water rose during the night."

This ingrate, whining for my paternal benevolence and plaguing me with his ridiculous problem. And right now, just when the boss is causing me unease and jumpy nerves (a transistor radio playing on his desk).

Now it's another day, discernibly different from the last.

I waited for the boss anxiously, in case he continued, this day, too, to be boss-plus-radio. And . . . no. He seems to have reconsidered his conduct.

Which made my own conduct immoderate, made me judge Besarión pitilessly, with rage and disdain.

———

Last night the big gray cat of my childhood came to me.

I told him that noise stalks and harries me.

Slowly, intensely, he cast his animal, companionable gaze upon me.

Besarión believes he knows everything.

He says it was the cat who interceded with the gods on behalf of mankind.

I probe deeper. "You accept that as true."

"No...Those are ancient beliefs. Paganism."

I set a trap. "I dreamed about you. In the dream, you were the intercessor."

He doesn't disparage this dream I've now lied to him about. He feels useful; he talks.

"I don't know. I don't know if it would do any good for me to intercede. When the moment comes, I'll make the request—and ask nothing for myself."

"What is it you'll request, from whom?"

"Don't interrogate me. That's not right."

———

"These *ballerina* shoes were made for you." This sentence formed in my head and I acknowledged, not without a certain smugness, that it might make for a pretty good ad campaign.

In shopwindows downtown, mannequin hands, like ivory but rose colored, hands without arms or body, hold a shoe made of supplest leather.

Ballerina shoes, these docile, delicate slippers, were created for her, for Leila, who does not wear them, nor perhaps even need them, as she circulates along the sidewalk across the street with the soft, light steps of a barefoot girl making harmonious movements with her body.

She waves at me.

I wave at her.

She joins her friend Nina. Then they talk about me. I know it: they both looked at me at the same time, trying not to lift their eyelashes.

Now they take up a different subject, with vehemence, and the discussion involves their hands. Surely this has nothing to do with me: they may speak of me but have no reason to argue over me.

Nina goes inside, apparently in search of evidence. Leila stays outside and her eyes glance back at me, perhaps to check if I'm witnessing all this. From inside, through the window, comes Nina's argument: it's dance music.

Nina reappears and Leila shows her how it's done. Nina sketches out her opinion of the twirls and footwork while Leila laughs, her hand not quite covering her mouth. Nina stops and stands, immobile and confused. She has neither rhythm nor musicality. She loses.

Which makes me sympathize with her.

I haven't wanted to risk pronouncing the magic number: seven days have elapsed without a bus or a bus's engine. Now I can embark on the adventure of saying so.

I have been disciplined in this resolve by Besarión. Yes, I've listened to him, and he says, "When the things we fear move away from us, they'll return if we name them. They'll mistake the mention of their name for a call to come back."

This turns simple fear into superstitious fear. Still, I went along with it because I cannot carelessly expose myself, and it's just for this once. From now on, I'll have no need of this apprehensive rule.

"Mamá, they're not bothering us anymore."

I said it cautiously, without indicating who or what. She knows.

"They haven't been waking me up anymore. Maybe they went away."

"Maybe."

"Do you hear them when I'm not here?"

"No, I don't."

She replies, but no more than that, offering nothing of her own. She doesn't join me in rejoicing over our recovered serenity. As if she weren't on my side. Which strikes me as odd.

The sound of the doorbell comes to the rescue, as if my mother had sent out an appeal for other things to require my attention.

It's Besarión, who never asked for—nor received—my reaction to the slip of paper he sent.

I won't react now either.

We walk awhile. But suddenly, as if obeying a summons, he decides to go home. He indicates that I can come along. It's early still: I go with him.

In the middle of the courtyard, as if in a boundless desert, stands his mother, her hands joined in supplication, calling out loving diminutives.

Her two canaries have flown away. Someone opened the cage.

"Did you go out? Did you leave the door open?" Besarión inquires.

"Yes, for a moment, just to the corner."

The crown of a tree rests against the rooftop. Two canaries linger in its branches, delaying their final flight.

I ask for a hose, and it's as long I need. I climb the wall and try to soak them. One escapes, but I douse the other, and it loses its nerve. I step onto the roof and capture it; the little creature barely resists.

I endeavor to communicate this triumph to the señora. She's signaling me desperately: in the hallway, something bad . . .

I scramble down the zinc roof, hose and canary in my hands.

Below, Besarión and the landlord are saying inflamed, bitter things to each other.

I direct the water against the wall. It hits, rebounds, spurts out in all directions. They aren't drenched; I just splash them, nothing more.

Enough to distract them from their quarrel.

His mother has contrived a modest reward: a pot of tea and some homemade cookies.

She serves us, then goes back to the kitchen where she's drying the damp, rescued bird next to the hot coals.

At this point my prudence grants me permission to speak.

"Besarión, the two of you should move out."

"I've thought about that."

"You have to. Will you?"

"Of course not. For a family, moving doesn't mean not having a roof over your head, it means exchanging one roof for another. But where is there another roof for me? How would we get one?"

A roof...

The title of my book about helplessness will be *The Roof.*

I talk to Nina. Lately something is making our paths and schedules coincide.

"It seems as if you're not in school anymore. Do you have a job?"

We walk along. Is she allowing me to join her or is she following me? She accepts my statement in a quiet little voice. "Yes, I have a job." And smiles.

I stop. I can't light my cigarette while walking. Nina waits.

She mentions Leila: the two were in high school together.

I understand why I'm standing here with Nina: she's Leila's friend.

"Do you have to work?"

"Oh yes! In my family, everyone wants to eat, wear clothes, lots of other things . . ." She laughs.

I like hearing her say it so merrily.

"Papá left us a house, but it's rented out. On very poor terms, unfortunately."

"Then where do you live? Do you rent?"

"Yes, but we'd rather live in our own house. We pay more in rent than our renter pays us."

I walk along in silence. She starts to sing very softly. I glance over at her. That makes her nervous, and she stops singing.

She reopens the conversation.

"You don't have a father either?"

"No. Not now."

Her gaze, though respectful, lets me know that she doesn't understand.

"I don't have a father now, though I had one, of course. He left us something, too: some property out in the country that we can't maintain, and a piano that stands in the dining room and never makes a sound."

"You and your mother don't know how to play?"

"No."

"I could come over," she proposes in sudden jubilation.

"You can play?"

"A little. Hardly at all. But I could make some noise."

What a stupid thing. What a stupid thing to say. Make noise just to make noise, and on a noble instrument. I grow indignant and abstain from further discussion.

At this she becomes absorbed in a little song, so soft it's barely audible.

"Why are you singing?"

"When I've done something wrong or feel sad, or when I'm with someone who doesn't talk, I sing."

Poor little Nina.

———

They're building an industrial shed.

My mother knew. She talks to the neighbors and frequents the grocery store. She hasn't betrayed me: her silence has protected me for many days, for as long as it could. Don't let him find out about it yet, don't let my son realize.

But today they arrived and there they are now, invisible and resonant, unloading iron tools and sheets of zinc.

As they nail, rivet, and pound, as that thing grows, I ponder how best to prevent it.

I thumb through the Civil Code. Something remains of the required readings from my student days, something vague: "Article 3096.—In the servient easement of runoff from adjacent rooftops, it is incumbent upon the owner of the dominant roof..."

If they build higher than my roof, the rainwater that falls onto theirs will run off to mine, which creates obligations for them. What obligations? "To maintain and clean the gutters and roof tiles." I'll have to watch out for that.

And their use of the wall? I notice they are using it for support. Can they? No. The code says no, because there's no reason to suppose it is a party wall: it doesn't run between two adjoining buildings but gives onto a kind of immense courtyard or long-vanished corral. Article 2719.

Yet if I were to say to them, "Señores, you cannot," their lawyer would simply whisper in their ear, "Purchase the undivided portion of the party wall. Article 2736." And since the law does not allow me to refuse to sell—*article ut supra*—for a few pesos they'll have acquired rights to the wall and will also have revealed me as an enemy, or, at least, someone who opposes their interests.

And I won't do that because I'm indirect (for example, I love Leila, but talk to Nina). Which in no way impugns my integrity. It is simply my method.

Nina has had no promises, commitments, nor words of love from me. But she follows me, she's developed an attachment to me.

That isn't at all how Besarión proceeded.

Besarión took a very trusting girl under his wing and she fell in love with him. In his own way he gave her lessons.

He didn't tell her, I love you, but neither did he say, I don't love you.

"I tell her," Besarión has explained to me, "that I'll be waiting for her on a given day, at a given time, in a given place. She doesn't ask why. Then she shows up, but I don't.

"Afterward, she says, I waited an hour for you. I guess I must have been waiting in the wrong place, or else you couldn't make it.

"You weren't angry with me? I ask.

"No. Why?

"Then I let her in on the truth. That way, she's forearmed. From now on no man will be able to deceive her."

Nina knows how to ask why, and she certainly would ask

if I were to make a date with her in a plaza or a tearoom. But I don't.

On the corner where our itineraries converge, the glowing tip of my cigarette sometimes winks at her.

We walk side by side to the front door of her house, where the light in the entryway shines far too brightly to allow for any attempt to beguile.

She tells me little things. She's a homebody, good-hearted. She'll spend her one free morning, Sunday, making sweets for her mother.

She talks about Leila. She must also talk to Leila about me. Tomorrow she'll tell her, "He's a writer." Because tonight I've confided that I'm working on a book.

If I were living in peace, I could have held that back. Before writing a book, I would never under any circumstances have said to a single human being that I'm a writer.

All I know about the industrial shed are the noises its construction makes and the purpose it's being built for. Information gathered by my mother indicates it will be an auto-repair shop.

I don't see it, I simply endure it. Since its construction will inevitably be followed by its operation, I try to find out what things are inside an auto-repair shop, so as to know what the sources of its future noises will be.

There's another repair shop along my way to work. When I walk by, it feels as if someone is vociferating through a megaphone and hurling cascades of screws and bolts at me.

I go inside to look around.

Immediately my ears defend themselves with a blockade of deafness, as if we'd entered a vast bell, very poorly cast.

No one takes any notice of my intrusion. The mechanics are vivisecting motors, sometimes beneath the wary eye of the garage's owner. They give a recently rebuilt engine a dry run, accelerating to make the machine roar, activating a release valve that injects gasoline in a series of explosions...

Those things over there, I tell myself, must be the worst: hammers brutally wielded against fenders, pounding relentlessly, transforming them to restore a shape distorted in some collision...

This must be what auto-body workers do, I reason, with a slight feeling of wonder at how many things we can easily name, even as we lack all knowledge of their mechanics. Such as rubber stamps. How is a rubber stamp made? It must be very simple, but I've never seen it done, nor can I imagine the system.

"You. What you want?"

I'd grown distracted to the point of forgetting myself. Here, where the human imagination seems to be inventing new noises on the spot.

"You looking for something?"

When vulgar words are flung my way, I fear the people who say them. It's as if no rational thought lay behind them. (If I speak them myself, I don't notice.)

"No, not looking for anything. Just looking."

"Looking. At what?"

"The work."

"You an inspector?"

"No."

"So...?"

"I'm a writer."

"A writer. You going to write something bad about us?"

"No."

"Oh really? Because some guy who lives back over there goes around threatening us with the newspapers. He's a clever one."

And he squares off at me again.

"So, what are we in here, anyway? A park, the cemetery, the train station?"

"I didn't think it could hurt to come in and take a look."

"All right, look all you want. After all..." And he walks away.

I'm a repeat offender. Once again I've said I'm a writer.

Leila is floating around across the street.

She doesn't dispense with me entirely. She greets me with a wave of the hand, and it seems her lips even form a word or two, words of greeting. But she doesn't look at me the way I think a writer should be looked at.

"Nina, do you tell Leila about things?"

"Yes, we're like roommates."

"Did you tell her I write?"

"No."

She modulates her voice. "Where you're concerned, I don't let her in on things."

"She wants 'in'? She tries, she asks?"

"No."

"She doesn't ask why we sometimes come down the street together and stand for a while at the door of your house?"

"No."

"No? She doesn't think it's important?"

"No. She thinks I'm going to ask for a job."

"Ask who?"

"Ask you. For a job in your office."

"Are you going to do that?"

"No."

"Then why do you put up with me?"

"Because you're good and decent."

"I'm good and decent?"

"Yes. And I'm alone."

"Alone? With your big family?"

"Yes."

"And with a friend like Leila?"

"Yes. Even with Leila I'm still alone."

I don't know what I'm going to do about Nina.

They've finished with the roofing.

It's Saturday and they're celebrating.

They're grilling meat—I can smell it—and they're full of high spirits, which is causing further deterioration to my state of mind.

I wonder what the flesh of the martyrs must have smelled like as they were burning at the stake.

My mother and I have lunch without speaking. We listen to the party.

My mother suggests I leave the house for the afternoon, maybe go to the movies.

The doorbell rings. It must be Besarión. I go.

It's Nina, with Leila. What? Without any warning?

"Am I . . . are we bothering you?"

"No . . . Of course not."

"Leila knows how, and I thought . . ."

"Knows how to do what?

"To play the piano."

Naive, generous, daring Nina.

Leila takes over the dining room. She registers all the things that have been placed on the furniture over the years. She picks up a few small pieces and shakes them like rattles, waiting to hear their inner voices.

She's never been this close to me or for this much time.

She doesn't speak; she's undertaking a kind of inventory of all our old decorations.

I couldn't say whether I approve.

Suddenly she leaves everything immersed in its former stillness to advance upon the instrument and say, smiling at me like an old pal, "This is the piano?"

The sudden introduction of such cheeky familiarity between us keeps her rather surprising question from irking me.

She opens the lid, plays a few chords, does some scales, and now it belongs to her.

It isn't the kind of music I would have chosen, but . . . There she is, and her presence alone brings me something I've hungered for, the good life I've never yet managed to grasp.

And Nina . . . ? She's still there, watching me look at Leila. Does she understand?

My mother brings in coffee and is glad. She's thinking that for a little while at least I've forgotten all about the party back there, with its smoking grill and general jubilation promising even more noise to come. She's mistaken. Not for nothing did I close the door between dining room and courtyard: it was to hide from Leila my shame at inhabiting a house that has been invaded.

Nina asks a question about the portrait. "Is this your husband, señora?"

I'm pleased that she says *is* and not *was*. These small courtesies are a comfort to my mother.

Leila does not follow her along this path of courtesy: if we have a piano in the house, but no pianist, it must be that we once had a pianist.

Instead, she feels called upon to share her thoughts about the instrument.

"It's old and a bit ugly, but I like it. I like everything about it: the sound, the ivory keyboard . . . But mine . . ."

"I've heard it," I interrupt, eager to show how close I am to her.

"You've heard it. How?"

"Many times, when you're taking lessons or practicing with the window open . . ."

She says "Ah . . ." as if allowing the subject to lapse. Or perhaps we've worn her out and now she wants to be entertained for a while, since she complains, as if not wanting to miss some program, "How can it be that you *still* don't have a television?"

She's brought up the very latest invader, and her *still* displaces us, disqualifies us, alludes to our tardiness in adopting the thing that everyone likes, the thing that has conquered everyone: the hypnotic device!

My mother asks, with a look, how she should respond. Not the truth, of course, which is that I've denied her this distraction so as not to go on accumulating more sources of noise in my home. While she does have a radio, that is thanks to my father, not to me, it dates from my boyhood; she only listens to it when she knows I'm not home.

My mother knows to answer "No, we don't have one," with a smile that seems to say everything without actually clarifying anything.

Leila appears satisfied with this explanation.

After that they leave.

Leila says goodbye to us; Nina says sorry to me, and I say, to Nina, "Thanks."

———

It's a Sunday, transparent and muted.

Yesterday's air brought word that spring would soon be making its rounds, but today an icy hand—perhaps ephemeral—grips the city.

Still, the sky is clear and the sun is doing its best against these last gasps of winter. I go down to the street around noon.

Leila is leaving for Mass, along with her maiden aunt.

Just the sight of her, that alone, warms my soul.

The cathedral is nearby and when she comes back I'll be walking along her sidewalk. It's difficult to predict, but perhaps she'll slow down and spend a while with me, walking together for a stretch, until she's called to the table.

Meanwhile, I pace up and down the block.

There's already a sign over the entrance. AUTO REPAIR. CAR WASH & LUBE. Through there, go in through there, and you'll reach the back of my bedroom ...

At least it doesn't say AUTO-BODY REPAIR.

It's noon, almost.

Leila, with her maiden aunt, is coming home from Mass.

She hasn't taken off her mantilla, and its whiteness, and an air of almost mystical serenity, heightens her glowing youth.

If she were part of my household, I think, I could devote time and still more time to observing her in repose, following her every languid move.

She bids me buenos días and keeps walking, arm in arm with the aunt, which seems to foretell that she, too, will grow old without a man at her side.

Why did I think that? Was it some visual intuition, or did it come to me out of pure humiliation? Why did she say buenos días, forgetting she already gave me that greeting on her way to Mass? Because I make so little impression on her.

Nina—for me, like an apparition—is suddenly there, and no doubt observed the slight.

I endure mankind's perpetual subjugation to the gaze of others. Only Nina's eyes don't verify: they hope.

The early afternoon sun licks at my window. No noise comes from behind it. The headboard of my bed is a bookcase full of novels, some inherited from my father, some selected by me. I accept their contagion. Perhaps today is the day I'm meant to begin writing my book.

I have almost all of it in my head. All that's left is to choose the point of departure. What do I say first? Where do I begin?

Sitting at the desk, I ponder this, and already the creatures I've conceived of do what they must do, living out the drama prefigured for them. I've told them to get moving and they move. The magic of my thoughts fills me with wonder.

I lean my head back and drift off. I'm happy and deserve this rest.

It's teatime. In my home, not in my book.

I respond to the aroma's summons and resolve to write later, until dinnertime.

Appeased by the warm herbal infusion, the sweet pastries, I become two, as midafternoon circles: I chat about something with my mother while the kernel of mystery that Besarión is creating goes round in my internal labyrinth.

He says he has a power and a mission. He doesn't use the power to solve even the most trivial problems, as if keeping it in reserve for a higher cause. And of the mission, he lets be known only that it will be impersonal and self-sacrificing. Is it, I ask myself, something like a self-immolation, the capacity to destroy himself for the greater good? Or perhaps not to destroy himself, but simply to destroy, in the belief that he can thus destroy evil.

Afterward, I don't write. I let myself be. My attention wanders.

———

Is it wind, trapped inside a tube that pitches the tone higher or lower according to the intensity of its rage?

No, it's water, a powerful, variable jet, perhaps propelled by forced air; it emerges with a hiss and disperses when it hits the metal.

The ablution, the first ritual.

They're washing cars with some machine that sprays water. Thus does morning and, with it, the repair shop's first job, begin.

At noon, they're still washing cars.

I come home at eight p.m. Soon it's ten thirty. They encroach upon every hour of the day: the legal working hours, the reasonable hour for lunch. They seem to have abandoned themselves entirely to their passion for the hygiene of all that has four wheels and an engine.

It's cold but my head is burning.

*

In the morning, before I leave—their daily tasks generally begin at seven—they're not washing any cars. Nor at noon. They're there: I can hear their conversations, now devoid of exuberance, as if they were restraining themselves.

"Maybe they won't get much work," my mother ventures. "They seem to be a small operation."

"They're new and obviously still unknown. But people will find them. The sign on the door is enough. They'll build a clientele."

I'm stubborn in my refusal to speak a word of hope, though inside I do have some hope, a hope against hope that the business will fail.

In the evening, I acknowledge the possibility that Nina is holding back, waiting for me, but I avoid the spot. I don't know whether today, again, the repair shop will destroy the peace I crave at my dinnertime and afterward, and I would be incapable of saying anything on a perfunctory or neutral topic.

The search for the right key among all of them—my mother, out of an abundance of caution, locks up early—becomes a trying task. I realize that anxiety is destroying me.

I open the gate to the courtyard. The shop's zinc roof is dark.

I need to sleep. I will sleep, a lot. Until seven the next morning.

If it weren't for the noise, I wouldn't have these memory lapses. If I hadn't forgotten some papers, I wouldn't have gone home in midmorning to get them. If I hadn't gone home at that unusual hour, I wouldn't have known, as I now do, that they also repair loudspeakers, producing squawk after squawk to check tone, intensity, and volume, sometimes mimicking the soundtracks of popular films as they do this.

My mother was spending her days under a bombardment of loudspeaker blasts. I fled.

That night I flee again, going straight from the office to the restaurant, though it's early still. While I wait, I have a vermouth. Two.

A few of us who were very friendly at school get together from time to time. We toss whatever's happened to us between one dinner and the next onto a kind of common discard pile, along with a reproducible flight of fancy or two. Lately we've also started bringing along other guests, perhaps to save these gatherings from the strain of our own mediocrity. Any of us can bring someone, and the check, the guest's check, is shared among us all.

Gutiérrez introduces Reato, a journalist; Franklin presents Pastor Flores, a folk singer.

The musician is a man of some renown. His earliest records are older than any of us.

Reato might also be considered someone, but only a few people—myself among them—know who writes for the papers.

"A journalist? For which paper?"

"The best one."

And he names the daily paper that is most widely read and offers the most thorough coverage.

My conviction that I can write is not based on any contact whatsoever with writers, only with books. In school, a literature professor of mine was a writer; he never recognized me. In the neighborhood where I used to live, a gentleman with a full head of graying hair seemed very much like everyone else. After moving away from that street, I saw his picture in a magazine: he was Poet No. 3. The Second-Best Novelist once sat at this very table. The daily papers' calendars of events have sent me off to join temporary congregations formed to listen to half a dozen of the nation's other writers. But that's the extent of it.

So the sudden proximity of Reato, a man who writes, sets me on fire. I want to be seen. Therein lies my perdition.

I challenge Pastor Flores, who has bolstered his fame as a singer and guitarist with countless bottles of wine. I claim I can drink more than he can.

Some of the others keep a tally of glasses served and downed. The race lasts from the beginning of the meal to its end.

Well before dessert I've grown befuddled, but I know I've won, or will win.

I can still make out the meaning of a few phrases. Pastor Flores's words aim to diminish my victory. "He got ahead of me even before they brought out the cold cuts. Typical of a lousy drinker: start in hard on an empty stomach. Does he live nearby? You know you're all going to have to carry him home."

I agree.

The inaccurate—or perhaps simply false—account given to my mother when I was delivered home in the early hours of the morning seems to have established:

(1) That I enjoyed myself enormously, and because everyone was having fun, everything turned out fine.

(2) That I brought honor to our little gang by emerging victorious from a fierce competition.

(3) That as we took our leave, there was a slight incident, without consequences (which contradicts the first point).

I have no memory of the slight incident, but I do know it involved blows given and received. As might be expected, some parts of my face maintain a more vivid record of the night's events. Moreover, I note that an impulse towards violence still runs through me. I feel like a fighter.

Day has developed in my windowpanes; I'm in bed, and the shop's noise is behind me, but even as I hear it, my mind, my muscles, and my blood are still benighted and under the reign of Bacchus.

———

Besarión is at the door. My mother doesn't know if she should let him see me bruised and in bed. She leaves him out on the sidewalk and comes to confer. Let him in.

He comes in.

Entering the room, he makes a physical display of prudence. He glances here and there, then desists, as if to say, "I haven't been invited to see everything."

He remains standing—between my bed and the table that serves as my desk, there's an empty chair—and doesn't ask what happened.

"I came to see if you wanted to go to the circus."

"As you see, I can't."

"Well, it doesn't matter. Another day."

"The same circus?"

"Yes. I'm friends with the lion tamer. He invited me. Well, goodbye. I'm leaving."

"No."

"No what?"

"Don't go."

Now he sits down, without having been invited.

"Outside on the clothesline there's a jacket with a torn lapel. Did someone beat you up?"

"Yes. I hit back, too. I'm not sure who it was."

"Had you been drinking?"

"Yes."

I tell him the story.

"I didn't think you were capable of anything like this," he says.

"Why?"

"You don't seem like the type."

"Well, now you know. I'm the type. The truth is I did it to show off."

"No. You're like that jacket. You're all torn up about something."

"That may be true."

"You want to forget something. Drinking is a consolation. Other people choose eating instead; they stupefy themselves with food, grow fatter and fatter, become lumbering monsters, and thereby succeed in annihilating their sensibilities."

"Aren't you exaggerating my situation a little?"

"I'm not talking about you."

"I'm only worried about one thing: I can't do some work I decided I wanted to do."

"What kind of work?"

I respond with his own words: "Please don't interrogate me."

In the silence that followed, he and I should have done what Nina does: sing.

"Well, I'm going."

"I guess you'll be back sometime."

"Of course I'll be back. You're ill."

The afternoon free of obligations, my warm bed, my mother's care, all soften me and usher me into a sleep where noise seems to lose its malice.

When my head clears, night has fallen.

My mother, very silent and still, is watching over me.

She notices I'm back, switches on the little light, and wants to hear it from me. "Are you all right now? Will you have dinner?"

I say yes. I ask her for a book and some pillows to prop up my back.

She says she'll make dinner, then comes back in with her ancient radio and tunes in to the public station. She withdraws.

The full, harmonic voices of classical music discreetly remove the car wash's spurting hose into the distance. An admirable palliative, devised—and never mentioned—by my mother.

Which, even so, in no way succeeds in blinding me to its limitations: the public station doesn't always play classical music, the other stations rarely do. And the noise produced when the repair shop is testing loudspeakers cannot be blocked out, not even by the Choral Symphony's lush *tutti*.

I've been reading only a few minutes. Besarión intervenes.

"Were you listening to music?"

"Yes." I switch it off.

Then the noise breaks out again and Besarión glances around as if a partridge had suddenly been flushed from the underbrush.

Then he seems to grow distracted, adopting an irritated and oratorical air. "For urbanists, the main questions are: How can we keep the houses from obstructing the high-speed highway? Where do we park the cars downtown? How do we avoid an intersection of more than three streets and create an elevated crosswalk? How can we heighten the apparent size of a building? How can we situate the marketplace in closest proximity to the freight train, or the highway to the warehouse?"

"What are you talking about, Besarión?"

"That." He points to the wall where my bedroom ends.

"What's that?"

"It's an auto-repair shop, isn't it?"

"Yes."

"Do you think that if an urbanist plans or establishes a city or neighborhood without traffic problems and with all the right solutions for water, air, light, verdant spaces, interior and exterior comfort, and also aesthetics, but then allows an auto-repair shop to be crammed into the middle of a residential block—do you think he has truly created a home for healthy men?"

"No."

"Of course he hasn't. And you're going to develop a gastric ulcer."

"Me? Why?"

"Because all the organs are connected to the brain by nerve cords. Your brain is stressed and it's sending a current to the stomach; that current burns the stomach's inner wall. You'll see."

"You're making too much of this, Besarión! Who told you I'm stressed?"

"Those things back there: they don't make you jumpy, they don't make your heart race?"

I don't concede, perhaps out of decorum. "Yes, sometimes. I try not to pay much attention."

"You must be used to it. You've had to bear it for a long time."

"No, they moved in there recently."

"Isn't it exactly what I just said? There are no restrictions, no limitations. There should be! Over here, with no blaring noises in the air, let's have the residential zone, where you can listen to the birds sing; over there, let's have the sports stadiums and entertainment complexes, the places where people dance and have parties with amplified music; and farther off, within very well-defined boundaries, the factories and repair shops that produce noise, smoke, and fumes.

"Do you see the process? The war ends, and the industrial economy is transformed: great quantities of the machinery of peace go on the market. Set to work, the machines soon break down: they must be repaired. To repair or replace their parts, businesses, repair shops open. They have to be located somewhere, and no one regulates them, no one dictates where. Wherever they find the space. There are many of them. They take advantage of small empty lots between houses and blocks. The man who owns some land behind his house that once belonged to his parents or someone else further back sells it, and at a good price. What moves in is progress, but it's not where it should be, because everything around it is residential, and people can't sleep or eat or read or speak in the chaos of sound."

"You're right. Calm down."

"I'm right?"

Yes, Besarión is right: until May or June the house belonged to one of those families whose name has turned to ashes.

"And now?"

"To some people who used to have a bus."

"Are they superstitious?"

"How would I know?"

"You should know, it's in your interest . . ."

"Why?"

"Because of Cora."

"Who's Cora?"

"The wife of one of the mechanics. They live over there, don't they? The owners of the repair shop?"

"Yes. How do you know her name is Cora?"

"For you—or for me—this repair shop is hell. Pluto was the king of hell. Pluto's wife was Persephone, sometimes known as Cora. Averno was one of the mouths of hell. It gave off a smell of sulfur. Those people live in the mouth of Averno—that is, of the repair shop.

"Tonight, you'll take some sulfur and spread it on the front steps of the house. Every morning, Cora, the woman of the house, must be the first one up. When she discovers the sulfur on her doorstep, it will trigger an atavistic memory. She'll fear death and badger her husband to move away. The repair shop will go elsewhere and you'll be left in peace."

With a semblance of reasonableness and apparent truths, Besarión has strung together something so false I can't establish any logical defense for it.

"But what if she isn't named Cora?"

"Doesn't matter. She must be superstitious, even so."

I pull myself together. "Besarión, you're superstitious. And contrarian."

"I'm not superstitious."

"I don't understand. You can't defend yourself, not even from a couple that fills your hallway with running water, but then you devise this intricate maneuver to defend me, which I haven't asked you to do. Tell me: What am I to make of you?"

"Nothing. I no longer defend myself. The courtyard of the apartment is covered in little mountains of dirt and mud. An underground pipe burst. That gave the owner his pretext to come and bother us inside. He's torn up floors, dug under them. The pipes aren't being fixed. Some of the neighbors help out, letting us use their bathroom. For cooking I bring water in jugs."

"But emergency work must be done to resolve that. File a complaint with the Department of Sanitation or city hall."

"Yes, we've started the proceedings. It doesn't matter. The man has won. We'll soon be leaving. Mamá will go to my sister Luisa and I'll go to the other one, Inés. I'm going to educate her children. Don't worry about the company: I'll go on selling."

The education that Inés's offspring receive, I say to myself, will be an unusual one.

Nina tries out a reproach.

"I felt abandoned…"

I assume a tone of severity. "You must realize, Nina, that I'm not the sort of person who chooses to increase his commitments and responsibilities. As far as I'm aware, their number has not grown any larger of late."

It pains me to lash out at her with such a lack of compassion. It's necessary, but I can soften it. "In the past few weeks, it's felt as if all the difficulties in the world were weighing on my shoulders."

Nina doesn't respond. Nor does she sing.

We're walking and there's still quite a long way ahead of us.

I say, "I'm in a hurry because I want to have dinner and go to the movies."

She says, "I could do that too."

I say, "Of course you could."

She says, "With you." And though the streetlights' dim radiance is tangled up in the branches overhead, I can see a young woman's eyes seeking my gaze.

"Nina, I love another girl."

"I know."

"If you know, then do you know who the girl I love is?"

I've paused very emphatically as I asked the question, which is a kind of invitation. She understands, and her answer is neither hasty nor uncertain.

Finally she says, "Maybe if I made an effort I would know."

At her door, thinking it's all over, I say a final adios. But she answers, "See you tomorrow."

During intermission, the idea of a cigarette draws me out to the lobby, where I see the journalist from the dinner.

I'm about to approach him when a murky impulse restrains me. I got into a brawl that night, or someone got me into a brawl. I don't know who it was and haven't been able to find out. Perhaps, given my sudden affinity for the journalist, and the reckless pride it gave me, I attacked or insulted him.

A mistake.

Reato sees me and waves from afar.

It's up to me to seek him out, and I do.

With a matter-of-fact gesture, he tells me the name of the man he's with. Then, taking me by the arm in a friendly way, he says, "If my newspaper weren't so stodgy and had a column just for laughs, then you, my friend, would already be inscribed in the minor history of alcohol and folk music."

"How's that?" I ask cheerfully, though I understand.

The theater's buzzer interrupts us. Reato gives me a pat, claims, "You know, you know," and excuses himself. "I'm off now, I'm off. This movie has to be seen from the very beginning... or even from before the beginning," and he laughs.

I walk into the illuminated late-night pharmacy and step onto the scale, not because I expect news from the pointer—I weighed myself this morning—but because I'm indirect.

Then I go to the counter and ask for sulfur.

"Magnesium sulfate?"

"No... I don't think so."

"In bars?"

"It's got to be powdered."

The clerk gives me a small, white rectangular envelope with something compact inside that fills it out evenly.

"That's six pesos."

An inexpensive weapon.

"Give me two."

"This one and another?"

"No. Two more."

No further delay is required: winter's final efforts have stripped the streets of witnesses.

It's easy to go over there, easy to do it.

Only one thing intimidates me: the silence...

I don't opt for the mouth of Averno, which is all locked up. Instead I choose the stone stairs that Cora, if she's in a hurry to get up, will be first to walk out onto in the morning.

I tear off a corner of each envelope and sprinkle sulfur until I've covered the entire surface. I bend down to spread it out more evenly with my hand, then realize that means I will walk away with something like an accusation on my palms.

Instead I find a little stick and on top of the layer of powder I trace a large *M*, the *M* in the word *muerte*.

Now it's done and I'm home.

As I take off my shoes I see they're sprinkled with yellow. A brush quickly eliminates this warning that everything we do leaves a trace.

Now it's time to sleep. Or to wonder whether or not it's true that I am a decent man.

In the morning, my three portions at six pesos each have all been swept away and the sulfur is scattered across the curb.

My powder, intended to ward off noise, has been pressed into service, instead, to ward off dogs.

Cora's atavistic memory has yielded to the utilitarian order of things.

———

Nina's voice, over the telephone, comes to find me at the office.

"It's to invite you to a get-together, at my house."

"A get-together...?"

"Yes, it will be fun. Come. You'll like it. Leila will be there."

"Leila will be there?"

"Yes."

"Why did you tell me that?"

"Because she'll be there, for sure."

"Fun? Will there be dancing?"

"There may be some dancing afterward."

"When is it?"

"Today, or, I mean, tonight. Can you make it? Will you come? Can we count on you?"

"That's very short notice."

"Short notice?"

"Short notice to learn how to dance between now and tonight."

"That's the first time I've heard you make a joke. It's funny! We'll have fun with it tonight. Have to go now. I'll expect you at nine. Be there!"

And she hangs up.

Curious effect my jokes have: they're not laughed at when made, but will be lots of fun ten hours later. Also, it wasn't a joke.

In any case, I didn't say I would go. Her interpretation is not my decision.

Besarión stopped by early and asked permission to leave me a brief note. My mother provided him with paper and ink in my bedroom, which is where my writing desk is.

On Saturday, if it doesn't seem like a bad idea, I'm inviting you to the circus again. If you accept, we'll have dinner that night.

We have water again at my house. (That's not what I want to celebrate.)

As I write you, it sounds as if a great battle is underway back there between the medieval era (iron against iron) and the twentieth century (engines). I know: it's just the repair shop, doing its work.

If in the end you don't sulfur them, you must be somatotonic (given to action and therefore predisposed to noise) or else viscerotonic (sentimental, sociable, and tolerant of noise).

Stravinsky and I are cerebrotonic (intellectuals who cherish solitude and silence). Stravinsky works in rooms with padded walls that keep the noise out.

From your room, I can see the clothesline where the jacket with the ripped lapel was hanging. I remember it gave me an image of you: a man torn apart. Though I don't know what tears at you.

Søren warns that a life torn asunder leaves man in a region of contact with the divine.

I have more sales calls to make. See you Saturday.

Did I write too much?

Far too much. And offensively.

Today, everything is repeating itself. Nina is celebrating, and Besarión is celebrating too, or wants to celebrate. In my bedroom, on the writing table's black blotter, lay the white slip of paper with the note from my friend. At the office, on my desk's olive-green blotter lies a white card with an invitation from the general manager. He's celebrating too.

The date is today, tonight. Somewhat disoriented by all

that is piling up on top of Nina's get-together, I go in to see my boss, card in hand.

The question is in my face and before I say anything he issues his directive. "You have to go. He's invited all the managers and assistant managers."

It wasn't me he invited but the assistant manager.

I allow myself one cavil. "But to send it at the last moment..."

"He says it's so no one will go to any trouble, so there won't be time to buy gifts. Nevertheless..."

Nevertheless, the collective gift—from the managers and assistant managers—is currently being acquired: someone's been delegated to go out and make the final arrangements. It will be deducted from our paychecks at the end of the month.

The white dress shirt, the black suit, the shoes polished to a high gloss, the silk socks...

My mother provides them, in accordance with my father's rules. She rises to these occasions by evoking the fashions of her personal era of sociability.

Sitting on the edge of the bed, I roll the perfect smoothness of the silk up my cold foot, listening to the silvery legends of my mother's youth. Then, behind me, I discern an entirely new noise.

To capture it fully, I must follow it. It isn't explosive, it isn't sudden, it isn't sharp. A busy insect sounds like this. Except that it cuts off, and as it cuts off, it vibrates. And then begins again.

I must inform Nina of my other commitment (or obligation). In passing. I will exhibit my formal attire. Perhaps Leila will see me.

On my way out, I see a light on the shed's zinc roof. It

doesn't extend as far across the roof as my gaze does. It's centered on the newest noise, in the part of the shed that abuts my bed.

"You couldn't make it, could you?" says the telephone.

I'm about to ask who's speaking, but my internal circuitry already has the answer.

"You couldn't make it." She's paving the way for my belated excuse.

Nina's education could use a few lessons from the school of my friend Besarión.

"When I was on my way out last night I was about to let you know but then I lost track, I don't know why."

"I don't know why, really: I lost track," I told the general manager.

I've arranged for someone to go to Town A, 80 kilometers from the capital, and then for a different person, for similar reasons and without great urgency, to go to Town B, 100 kilometers away. But Towns A and B lie only about 25 kilometers from each other.

Because of me, the company has displaced two men who will cover a total of 360 kilometers. If the man sent to Town A had been ordered by me to go from there to Town B and then come directly back, the second man could have been doing something else and the sum total of kilometers covered would have been 205.

I've learned that a company cannot comprehend distraction (and a manager is a company). I add, "What alarms me in this matter is the neglect of geometry. Because between them, the capital and Towns A and B form a triangle, and the distance…"

He hears me out and tries to understand. His gaze says, "Well, this is an original excuse." For my part, I'm only saying whatever comes into my head, just as I was doing initially after I went in to see him.

When I came in, he inquired, fairly certain of the response he would get, "Did you enjoy the party?"

"Yes."

Both he and I observed that this was insufficient. Only then did I round it off with a further platitude.

"Yes, a great deal."

These things might not be happening without the noise. It's making me weak.

Perhaps because I'm feeling that way, a little weak, I can't seem to understand the other noise that has now arrived.

I don't know whether it's actually doing me harm. I do know that even if it isn't physically damaging me, it obsesses me, constricts me, weighs me down, as if thick, sticky nougat were spreading over my body.

I don't know what produces it, or why. When, in its punctual way, it cuts off, it lies and repeats the lie that it won't go on any longer. It always goes on.

I don't know what it is, but its perseverance makes me imagine it comes from a man chained to a machine.

———

Possibly because I'm in this state, I fall in with Besarión and his program. I haven't forgotten the slip of paper he left me, but now I can't seem to specify how or why it struck me as exasperating and erroneous.

He has me out of the house before night has fallen.

"The show won't start until nine," I object.

"We'll go to the wild animal show beforehand."

However childish that would be...

They haven't put up the tent for the animals yet. Besarión paces in front of the lot, smoking and paying no attention to me.

Do I wait for him to come back to earth? Do I leave?

A brass band with drums and fake uniforms, as if on military parade, squeezes past the kids who've been worked up by the delay and the yawning and roaring of the caged animals.

The tent is thrown open.

A few lions, skinny but majestic, and an admirable leopard, not yet resigned to its fate, justify the big sign that promises WILD ANIMALS. The rest are miniature horses, zebras, monkeys, parrots. And flies, too, flies that probably have a very easy time reproducing in the smelly straw lining the cages. They assail us mercilessly, like the vengeful guardian parasites of the animals held back by the iron bars.

Besarión dodges them, waving his arms around. His mood darkens.

"If it's all right with you, let's get out of here," I suggest.

"Soon," he says, making an effort to move ahead.

A girl slips between the cages. I observe that the lions, indifferent to us, all gaze at her. She's small, and her body in motion has the vital elasticity of a leather whip.

The kids are pushing me, and I take a few steps forward.

I've lost track of Besarión. When I look around, I find him behind me, talking to the girl.

Then she leaves and he calls me over to the exit.

"There's still half an hour. Would you like to eat?"

That seems reasonable. I say, "Sure, great."

He buys peanuts and nougat and invites me to share. Great...

Even so, Besarión takes none of a child's—or an adult's—pleasure in the circus.

I point out a cluster of four loudspeakers on the highest tent pole, which transmit cheap, tinny music devoid of all fidelity, along with a litany that goes, "In just a few minutes the greatest show of the greatest circus on earth will begin..." I add my note of sarcasm: "The cerebrotonics who live near the circus are most unfortunate."

In response, Besarión's bad mood tilts, for a moment, towards either clemency or fury, I'm not sure which.

I say, without any sort of ill will towards him, "I could help them by writing something. I know a journalist."

"What's your idea?"

"Nothing, but I could. Defend the neighborhood from the noise, the hours of braying loudspeakers, the terrifying roar of wild beasts waking them up in the middle of the night, the filth of all these neglected animals..."

"Don't do anything to the detriment of the circus. The lion tamer, his daughter, and the *écuyère* travel with it, and they need it."

"I don't understand."

"They're necessary to the Organization."

"What organization? The circus?"

"No. The other one."

There he is again, in his zone of obscurity. I fall silent and meditate. If I ask him what the Organization is, he'll lock down. I opt for an indirect approach.

"Besarión, can I belong to the Organization?"

"No."

"Why not?"

"You lack the vocation."

This line of questioning never leads anywhere with Besarión. What vocation? Vocation for what? Who determined that I lack it? Did he? By what secret means?

The lion tamer has some professional skills, or so it seems to me when he dominates the lions' snaggletoothed hostility.

Besarión has revealed that we'll be dining with him later on, which at least indicates that there will be dinner.

We're welcomed by a tavern, its nightlife barely in evidence at that hour.

In orange chalk, someone has written a code of conduct on a blue wall:

NO SINGING

NO CARDS

PENALTY: EXPULSION

(*No exceptions*)

"Why no singing?"

"To prevent fights. No one sings from happiness here. Anyone who starts in with that gives himself away: he's dangerously drunk."

These may be pure suppositions on Besarión's part. He's waxing encyclopedic again.

But in the lion tamer's presence he abandons his lucubrations, and the circus performer, without his colorful jacket, is subdued. From their conversation, I gain no information, nothing of interest, and no experience, since I'm only included briefly.

I'd like to hear him talk about lions and leopards, bears and tigers. Which is natural. But the lion tamer prefers to talk about his travels. Which is also natural.

Only one phrase, a question, conjures up an invisible context: "How's your French?" he wants Besarión to tell him.

The dwarf couple, the skinny individual with the nails, the Korean jugglers in their green pajamas, the (lame) contortionist who gives a little wriggle when she walks in, as if she were still performing, all share a table where a man in a hat is stationed. He signs and distributes some small, square pieces of paper, then gets up and hands one to the lion tamer who is dining with us. I glance over and see it's a voucher. This bit of paper gives the lion tamer his food, his living.

The man in the hat proceeds with the distribution, revealing, in various corners, the horse trainer, the antipodeans, the fire-breathing Hindu magician, the tightrope walker, and the trapeze artists who've momentarily stopped doing the stretches that seem indispensable to them whenever they're not flying through the air.

More or less the entire population of the big top. Which explains why Besarión allowed the lion tamer to select this particular establishment for our dinner.

There's no mystery. They aren't all there, either: the *écuyère*, who was pretty and could have been at our table, hasn't come.

There's no toasting of any kind with Besarión. Gloomy place for a celebration.

We return from this negative night.

I ask Besarión about his French and why he's studying it—simply for the sake of learning or to read something in particular?

"I'm studying French in order to speak to the French in their own language. I plan to go to Paris."

"To Paris, specifically?"

"Specifically to the Île de la Cité, where for eight centuries a church has stood, founded by the son of a woman who, like me, gathered wood."

"The cathedral?" I hazard.

"Yes. Notre-Dame. I have something to ask for—and not for myself."

"But way over there, so far… If you're asking the Virgin for something, you can find images of her everywhere."

"Don't meddle in this. The devotion of my commander requires that it be her."

"All right. But tell me straight-out: Is this the mission you've been talking about? Is this your mission?"

"No. Or rather, yes: one aspect."

"Is it or isn't it?"

"It is implied in the fulfillment of my mission."

I force myself to remain silent while something like a wave of anger surges within me. Then I stop, turn to face Besarión, and protest: "This can't be. You're getting me involved. What are you trying to do, make me admire you?"

He has stopped too; he hears me out, then answers at once, and severely, "You cannot bear witness. You won't do."

"Why do you use that kind of language with me?"

Besarión challenges me with his eyes, but I won't stand for being roped in or for his covering his tracks again. "Tell me one thing that's reasonable or plausible."

"For example?"

"It's quite a trip! Who's financing it: You? How? With what?"

"If I tell you, will you stop poking around in my business?"

"Maybe."

"Yes or no?"

"All right."

"Well then. Yes, it's an expensive journey, of course. Too expensive for me, as you well know. But not too expensive for the Organization, and the Organization is making it possible for me to go. Understand?"

Sunday's light is slowly dimming. Without Leila.

Tomorrow, when she's coming home from school, I'll try to cross paths with her.

My attention has wandered from Leila, and from my book...

I might regain possession of the blank fragments of my time if only Besarión would actually leave this city.

Careful not to flavor the information with any doubt or hesitation, I share with my mother what Besarión says he's planning to do.

My mother listens, then offers a parable.

"Your grandmother lived for seventy-five years, forty-six of them with your grandfather. When she died, he refused to acknowledge it. He kept to his room for several days, in deep depression, then seemed to pull himself together and went back to all his daily habits.

"But in the evenings, he'd grow restless and ask us to saddle up a horse for him. He didn't know how to ride a horse, we lived in a city."

"What did he want to do?"

"'Go and see her,' he'd say."

"Where?"

"In Sicily, in the village . . . But we were in America.

"We'd say all right, and take him out to the car for a long drive. He'd calm down.

"When he got home, we'd ask him about Mamá.

"'She's fine, she's happy. She doesn't want you to worry,' he'd reassure us.

"'So you saw her?'

"'Yes. I went to Italy, to our village, on that black horse out there in the street.'"

I think over my mother's little story.

Then I try to outline my position.

"I've come to believe, last night especially, that Besarión suffers from some kind of hierarchy disorder."

"What is a hierarchy disorder?"

"Is it hard to understand? It's the only description I can come up with. He feels himself to have forces, powers, to be carrying out enormous orders or instructions, of what kind I don't know: spiritual or material. He thinks he's meant to exist on a higher plane, but life has kept him very low. This latter fact he doesn't seem to perceive. If he's aware of it at all, he tries to deceive himself, not see himself as he really is. So he moves between two worlds, two different orders of things."

It's not clear, either, whether he's guided by love of others or love of himself. He doesn't appear to occupy himself much with other people, but it's possible that without saying to anyone in particular "I'm here to help you," he's thinking of everyone.

My mother is also indirect.

"In every school, the students who behave well are rewarded with good grades. Isn't that true? And in some schools, the incentives may vary according to the teachers' imaginations: special prizes like colored pencils, a globe, a doll, a bracelet... In my boarding school, the Mother Superior invented a costume and a ceremony for the girl who distinguished herself by her generous character, good conduct, and religious devotion. She would dress her as an angel and place a chorus of angels around her, made up of other girls who had previously shown themselves to be as good and as disciplined as she was."

With a smile, I'm the one who voices the conclusion: "And I am putting an angel costume on my friend Besarión—that's all."

My mother smiles and underscores my words. "That's all."

"No," I argue, this time in all seriousness. "Because I also think the opposite. If in place of *love for others*, I put the words *harm*, *vengeful malice*, or any other definition of wickedness, or if instead of *self-love*, I posit a desire for self-punishment, the mechanism that moves Besarión still works the same way."

I pause because I'm about to change my tone and say something very different. "That's what I used to think, because I never stopped scrutinizing him, always a little fearful of his effect on me. But from now on I don't think it's right to analyze him. I won't ask myself whether he's lying or telling the truth."

Then—because Besarión's fundamental problem is not noise but housing, though he takes on the noise problem in my stead, while I hide it and deny that noise torments me—I go on: "He insists on buzzing around here. Something drives him to come. All right then, let him come. If he doesn't get on my nerves too much, I'll let him go on with his palpitations and meanderings, and see what comes of it."

I'll observe him, an impassive witness, as if he represented all the aspects of life that we endure without understanding.

The iron rim of a wheel startles me awake Monday morning. I know the procedure well: they stick a crowbar into the rubber that surrounds the metal, then pound it with a hammer or some other iron implement until the tire hugging the metal rim is forced off. The noise doesn't stop until the rim has popped out, rolled around crazily, circled in place awhile, and come to rest on the pavement.

Then, inside the shop, the long intermittent hum starts up again.

What is it? What's it doing? Is it reeling up a very strong filament? Pulling and, as it pulls, engaging a set of metal teeth? And when it reaches the end, does it clamp down, grind, bite, or crush with a force that runs back down through the coiled filament to the teeth?

If I knew something about the process, I might also know whether the machine had been installed permanently, to stay there and grow old behind my back.

I go looking for the noise, that continuous noise, in the other auto-repair shop that is neither a cemetery nor a train station, but lacks discretion: its sheds extend to the edge of the sidewalk and stand wide open.

My plan is to acquire knowledge simply by listening and comparing. I approach every machine and every mechanic whose activities have sonorous results I'm unacquainted with.

I make inquiries, try to describe it. With my index finger I draw the reeling in of the sturdy filament in the air. And fail to come up with a single lead. I can't seem to make anyone understand me. "Why do you want to know?" a machine operator who's grown weary, or wary, of me interjects at last.

An encounter with schoolgirl Leila is not wholly alien to my intentions, but I leave that up in the air. Better to head home before the hardware store closes; I require the loan of a ladder and a man to help me carry it.

The repair shop sometimes takes a break, though never for more than half an hour. I can tell from the withdrawal of sound, the void it leaves, the way that void immediately overflows with silence.

As soon as the wave of peace declares itself, I clamber hurriedly up the ladder that I set up earlier with the assistant.

I proceed across the zinc, which is no easy thing: it is undulating, slippery, and steep. No one sees me: I'm crawling on hands and knees.

I reach the opposite side, where my house is. Down there, just ahead of me, the workshop discloses all the areas I've been guessing at. I'm not there to make a general survey, only one specific discovery: the source of the new noise that occurs so frequently.

Whenever it happens, the sound is right next to my wall; to see it my gaze must travel straight down, which makes me dizzy. I manage to overcome that and make out, in the corner, an instrument that looks something like a carpenter's bench, though it's short and metallic. Whatever parts of it aren't gleaming, polished steel are covered in sky-blue paint. And that's it. I've failed. The device looks so simple, but I don't know what it is or what it's used for.

I climb down. My mother gazes at me. She can see that I've entangled myself in a spy scheme that does me no honor.

*

Nevertheless, I must learn what it is, once and for all.

In the phone book, I look up the names of services and stores that may be able to help me pin down the precise nature of that solid phantasm. I don't succeed, but I'm reminded that there's a street where all the businesses that deal in industrial machinery are lined up next to one another.

I do something that can only heighten the unease with which my boss views all those who fail to keep strict hours. I leave.

The street in question is, to all appearances, the ordinary place to go for any would-be buyer of the machine I seek. I pretend to be a buyer. I identify it, and confirm its insect-like sound, its vibrations, its spasms. I learn that it shapes pieces of metal.

I'm staggered to realize, at last, that the machine in question is a lathe. It's true that I had never seen a lathe, and that must be true of many people. But in any city, terms like *machinist* and *metalworks* abound, along with other indicators that, at an earlier time in my life, would have produced an immediate response in my mind.

At an earlier time in my life.

I return home. As I walk down my street, the part of the city that extends along it turns out the lights in its shopwindows, lowers its shutters, dismantles the scaffolding of its workday. Until tomorrow.

But there's one place where activity persists: behind my house.

The light is confined to the corner where the lathe is, the lathe with the consistent throb that I'm also beginning to detect inside my head, where one vein palpitates more than the others, with particular martyrdom, and hurts a little.

Dinner, though prolonged by morose table talk, doesn't last long enough to take up all the time the machine is demanding for itself that night.

I gather my gloves and scarf back up.

"You're going out? Now?"

"Yes, for a little while."

I walk towards the circus, simply to have someplace to go.

It's gone. The empty lot churns with shadows. Was it ever here? Was it here last night? I step on sawdust, wet and pasty, staying away from the holes that supported the wooden structure beneath the stands. For the next few days even the slightest gust of wind will entertain itself with empty caramel packets and torn wrappers from chocolate bars.

I think back on the tavern and have an overwhelming impulse to see what sort of peril or good fortune that establishment and its rules may have in store for a man from a different milieu.

The front door is ajar, while everything else is shut tight, though it's clear there's smoke and warmth inside.

My course is set. I go in.

The owner of the inn—the heavyset individual in an apron who emerged from behind the counter with some effort yesterday evening—has died.

I ask questions. "Of natural causes," I'm informed. Which is possible, as experience has shown.

My mood—oh, paradox that I am—is further stimulated.

But this does not prove contagious in the atmosphere of that room.

I view the dead man in his coffin, remitted to a small side room.

I read the gilded letters and little cards attached to the flowers. Almost all are from friends, signed, "Tus amigos." One is more explicit: "Adiós, Pancho. Tu amigo del alma, C. Clavel." Another is from his widow.

She sits, shriveled up in her black widow's weeds, in a chair near the side room. I take her hand and she thanks me. "Muchas gracias, señor."

She seems to address every one of her husband's patrons as *señor*. I suspect it's only now that she's coming to know something of the business that left her ignored, as wife and as companion, stranded in some room with a kitchen, far beyond these walls.

NO SINGING
(No exceptions)

Beneath the sign is an army of bottles, in strict formation. Tonight they stand there for friends, at no charge, to help us bear the cold and in memory of the deceased. I learn the procedure: all you have to do is walk up to the counter and say, "Let's see, a glass of..." and take your pick.

I go over and, in my own way, take my pick. "Do you happen to have a bottle of champagne?"

I speak of my mood and I speak of danger, but no one pays attention to my sallies, and the bartender, with the usual indifference of his kind, answers. "We don't have champagne. Anisette?"

There's a light on in the repair shop. Work is ... still going on. It's one thirty in the morning.

The vein in my head grows impatient; the throbbing keeps up its cadence.

I sit down on the bed.

I follow the laborious vicissitudes of the lathe, the short stretch that precedes the buffing of the metal, which comes before the pause, the brief respite that offers an instant of hope, having only just been born when it's already destroyed.

The breathing that emerges from my mother's room doesn't have the relaxed sound that attests to good sleep. If she's quiet, if she hasn't said a word, it's because she's afraid of influencing my decisions.

No, there will be no violence. I will not scream at them to stop, to leave, to let me sleep, to at least leave the night free for me. No.

I will be legal, precise, and implacable.

At the police station, the officer on duty listens.

"They must be working," he surmises.

I should tell him that if he's passing judgment rather than taking action, that's already a sign of his bias. But I refrain.

"If they're working at this hour, they are breaking the law. There is a time stipulated for that."

"For an employee. But what if the person operating the lathe is the owner?"

"Even if the owner is operating the lathe, this isn't the right time for that. This is the time for rest."

"So, what do you want us to do? You want us to make him stop?"

"Of course I do."

"If the repair shop is closed, that's not possible. We'll issue them a summons in the morning."

"Officer," I say, my voice shaking, knowing I'm making an enemy, "I am filing a complaint, and if you do not wish to be remiss in your duty, you must register the complaint and proceed. I demand that you at least order an immediate investigation of the facts."

With masked fury, he lends me a patrolman.

The man in a greatcoat with a shoulder cape accompanies me.

He's my only soldier, and the laws of war require that I know him to be fully on my side. I can't manage any sort of dialogue, though; he seems to have been snoozing when the officer called for him and now he's dazed and cranky.

I try to instill some notion of the torture I'm enduring. I instruct him in the delicacy of my daily labor and the need for complete repose at night.

"Police work is delicate too," he says.

"Of course it is," I say, coloring my assent with admiration. I don't know what he's preparing to argue, but my explanation has doubtless gotten through to him on some personal level.

"Sometimes we're on duty for forty-eight hours straight, like I am now. When it's my time to sleep, I need it more than you do."

"I see that clearly. I understand."

"I go to bed during the day. My wife puts the radio on and sings while she does the ironing; the old man is retired and has his TV on all day; my sister-in-law and her husband start fighting very early; the neighbor's brats come over to play with my kids in our yard; and I . . . I sleep all the same."

Well, there it is. The situation has been made clear and I now have advance notice of his position and his report.

At my house, he doesn't want to go any farther than the patio. "This is fine," he says. I stand motionless so nothing will keep him from hearing. He listens and says, "There's nothing to hear."

I take him by the sleeve of his greatcoat and propel him over to the wall. He obeys in astonishment, and his astonishment increases when he manages to distinguish the source of the disturbance I consider to be criminal.

At noon my mother, whose anguish is carving out a disoriented silence within her, has something to communicate. "Hijo, a policeman came. They've issued you a summons..."

"A summons to me? I'm the one who filed a complaint!"

But I present myself.

The owners of the repair shop have explained themselves. They had an urgent job and worked through the night in order to deliver the parts early.

"When did you speak to them?"

"This morning."

"Did they come here?"

"No. The sergeant went over to let them know you'd filed a complaint."

Now I'm exposed. For those people, I'm now the troublemaker, a threat. Before, their noise was unconscious, but from now on they can deliberately increase it to wound me and exact vengeance.

*

I go back to present myself again to my mother. I don't want her to spend the afternoon fearing I'm in trouble with the law or in jail.

She says, "We'll talk later. I think you should move your bedroom."

I say, "Yes, later," and wonder whether this small family that she and I comprise should move house altogether.

Today, at the company, Besarión has a moment of fame. The news travels all the way to my unit.

The secretary tells the boss, and the boss calls me over. "Besarión—you know, the salesman—has resigned. He says he's leaving the country. I say: deported!"

No, I won't laugh at my boss's humiliating joke. Let him go on laughing, let his eyes invite me to join in: I won't be part of it.

Nina's here.

I can't turn my back on her, but I'll defend myself in the following manner: "I haven't slept. I am the local resident who's had most contact with the police force since yesterday. And Besarión has given me a shock... Right now I'm not in any condition for the kind of calm, reasonable conversation you want."

No, I won't mount a defense. I'll accept her prudent reproaches, allow her prattle to lead me along...

No, not that either. Instead, I pay no attention to her. With a gesture I put a halt to her monologue and tell her that if I could simply manage to clear my head, there's no doubt I would think about her more.

It would appear that saying something like that is the beginning of something else, because Nina comes and stands in front of me, the more closely to monitor my next words.

I have no more words. What I need now is to kiss her, and we kiss.

When individuality returns, the sweetness of the encounter persists.

I will marry Nina.

That's the easiest thing. Yes, much easier than all the rest.

———

A six-armed instrument—the arms being mine, plus my mother's brother's, and a local handyman's—performs the quick move: my bedroom is relocated to the dining room, and the dining room is now where my bedroom once was.

The furniture mimics the prelude to a summer storm; the dragging of the dresser and hutch are rumbling thunder, and the bookshelf, recently emptied of its cargo, falls over with a loud bang and skids along the floor.

I've accomplished my flight, though I haven't eliminated the noise from the repair shop. I've only detached it from my immediate vicinity.

My mother remains exposed: her bedroom furniture can't be moved because there's nowhere else to move it. But she tries to spare me any remorse. "It doesn't bother me as much," she says, comparing herself to me.

Now I will sleep with greater protection. Besarión left, or will leave. I will marry Nina. Perhaps I can return to my book (can begin to write it).

I'll have to do without Leila. Things will be calmer that way.

When I feel a need for her, I'll tell myself she's a fictional creation, a child born of my second work. And someday I'll write that book, too.

Or rather, she'll provide the subject for a ballet libretto. I'll title it *Society Notes*. It will begin with the christening announcement in the Births and Babies column, move on to the dance that launches her into society at age fifteen, then continue under the rubrics of Engagements, White Masses (in celebration of medical personnel), Nuptials, and Travels. And then, long after her children's birth announcements, will come the listings in Illness ("Her condition is serious..."), and...

No. Let's leave it there.

———

"A radio?"

"Yes. They're listening to the race."

The Sunday paper said as much: a radio station will broadcast in its entirety a rally that ranges across the entire map of the country for some eighteen to twenty days.

I understand: They're people whose business is cars, and naturally they want to stay on top of every detail of the race. Even if, over here, it's all too audible, as if the radio were standing in the middle of my yard. They must have to turn the volume all the way up to hear it through the noise their work makes.

After a while my head feels overloaded with the names of people and places, with numbers: distances, speeds, cylinder capacities.

I take refuge in my bedroom. I can still hear, though it's somewhat muffled there, the combination of real automobiles being washed or repaired and invisible cars that, as recounted by the announcer's penetrating voice, chase each other down remote roadways, pulling ahead, rolling, crashing, killing someone.... Then they roar into the distance because their number is vast and the only condition of their existence is to advance.

Without argument, Nina allows me to place certain limitations on her calm enjoyment of becoming a betrothed woman: that her family not learn of it yet, that the wedding take place when I decide and tell her so.

The radio maintains its fidelity to the car rally.

My mother no longer puts her radio on, it's drowned out by the repair shop's.

At the table, we almost never speak. We have to listen; the radio subjugates us.

The abject state I'm in is due to the noise, and also to something I've decided not to share with her.

I've drafted a message to the mayor to register a collective complaint: continuous excessive noise; radio played at top volume, entirely unrelated to the nature of the establishment and its work; vibrating lathe with base attached to the wall of other houses (indicator of safety risk); inadequate enclosure of the upper sector of the shed's side walls and consequent emission of loud noise.

The nineteenth-century legal code, with its unfeeling ordinance concerning what it terms "noise nuisance," provides no sound basis for attack. But I twisted it to give my arguments the appearance of being duly invested with legality.

I visited the neighbors on one side, on the other, and in back. No one signed, no one wanted to join forces with me.

Some may truly fail to notice the noise. Others, though, are pretending, so as not to point an accusatory finger; either they fear conflict or don't trust or like me.

The dentist's wife tried to get out of it with a pleasantry. "My husband has a drill too"—is what she said.

The pharmacist opened his arms wide as if to receive me into them and soothe me. "This neighborhood is my life! I can't go around quarreling with people."

I mused with bitterness—and perhaps without justification—that if they don't mind having their thoughts disrupted, it's because they don't think much.

If I told my mother about this failure, I'd leave her even more alone: she'd be humiliated to know that these acquaintances are now keeping their distance so as not to have to support her son's petition.

"They're the living embodiment of mayhem!" the retired sergeant exclaimed in response to my request.

I admired his wrath, calculating that in any eventual combat I'd be no more than his shield bearer. "And they should watch out," he added. "You tell them not to get too far out of line, because one fine day I'm going to lose patience and go for my knife!"

Then his tone changed and he said, with finality, "But I'm not signing any papers. I don't like squabbling or lawsuits."

The touch of Nina's finger. "Why?"

Why can't she tell people? Why can't there be even the vaguest of dates, not a specific day or a month, but a year, an era?

I say, "Because I can't be sure."

"Of getting married? Of marrying me...?"

"I can't be sure of getting married."

Nina dissolves. Then comes her voice, with a little song.

She reminds me of a mad girl rocking back and forth with a doll in her arms, singing to it. I must have seen the illustration in some sad old almanac.

I ask for silence and she complies, and for half a block sustains it.

"I don't live well," I tell her.

The excuse isn't clear to her, though she tries to follow its meaning.

Then my case spills out, in all the chronological and circumstantial detail that will lead her to rethink things, to decide whether my noisy house scares her, to see in her future husband a vulnerable man.

She wraps herself around me, nestles against me. As if to say, "If they attack you, they'll find us together."

And that, it strikes me, is another image from an old almanac. But it moves me and offers a moment of certainty: I love this girl.

Passersby are looking at us. I yield to the dissociative power of their gazes and delicately disentangle Nina from my person.

We go on walking.

"Did you know...?"

"Not at all."

"I'm not seen as haughty, mean, pedantic, cantankerous...?"

"Don't imagine, querido, that everyone is judging you. And anyway, just let them try...!" and she extends towards the world her implicit threat.

From an evil action by A, H can deduce the universal nature of evil, and I will be implicated within it. From my evil action, A can deduce the universal nature of evil, and H will be implicated within it. But no one is absolutely evil within himself, even if he might be to others. Each of us has a justification. Which might not be accepted by others (except for those predisposed in our favor, those who love us).

The rally has ended. Even so, the radio stays on; they've grown accustomed to the sound of it.

It exhausts me, it shatters me, but I don't contest my mother's resignation. "At least what we're hearing now is music."

She doesn't entertain that misconception for long. Within two or three days, she's starting to look lost, even among her own things.

For my part, there's a constant pounding in my chest. Why? When it's only music...?

The alarming dimensions of my rancor lead me to reflect.

It isn't always music of the type I would have chosen. Sometimes we hear it when I feel like listening to music, but we also hear it when I don't feel like listening to music.

Therefore, yes, it's music, but it isn't chosen music. It's imposed music.

Music, which is sound, becomes noise when it is imposed. Imposed music.

In the same way, words from the radio or television represent nothing but noise when, as is usually the case, they have no meaning, or very little, or even if they do have meaning, it escapes me, because I'm listening to the words against my will.

Without my interest or acceptance, the TV becomes just noise with faces.

If the gentleman I share a seat with on the bus is reading a newspaper that I don't wish to read, his action doesn't affect me as long as he doesn't read aloud. If, instead of a newspaper, he carries a transistor radio in his hands and broadcasts a talk show that I don't want to hear, he causes the show to expand: it invades me, he imposes it on me.

I think about houses whose noise cannot escape their walls. Nor does their music, a music that will never be imposed on anyone.

The urbanists of all nations who, according to Besarión, are not disposed towards an antisonorous vision of the city, put their heads together, stand around my dispirited body, and strike a blow for sanity. "A house that blocks out all noise from outside can be built, though it's very expensive. But a house that entirely prevents any noise from escaping? Open a window, and out it comes."

I listen respectfully. When they've finished, I kick and squirm on the floor. I say, "I appeal."

"To whom do you appeal?"

"To someone who can make mankind better."

"So he doesn't make noise?"

"So man does no harm to man. Neither visible harm nor invisible harm."

"And if he does harm without knowing it . . . ? If he believes he's playing music, but what you hear is noise?"

"Oh"—in despair, I realize they're using my mind's own secret arguments against me—"in that case, then let a man's words be believed. Enough to raise a hand and say 'Don't hurt me' for the other to desist, understanding that to someone else, his spray of jasmine is a spear."

Sometimes I pull back from myself and think this way, in dialogue. But the intensity of these dialogues leaves me lacerated, as if they were real.

There, across the gutter, ten workmen have gathered to nail an incomprehensible platform into place, splicing the sidewalk to the paved street. Whatever the facts might be, and I felt no curiosity or compulsion to learn them, I envisioned this as a first step towards urban progress: the deep gutters, or acequias, that are characteristic of our city—something like irrigation ditches along our residential streets—should be covered so that careless women can't throw trash into them and children caught up in their play are protected from pitching into their dangerous, muddy waters.

The ten men return, or ten others like them; they erect wooden partitions more than two meters high over the platform they built a few afternoons ago.

The partitions form six cubes whose cover is a roof that arrives fully constructed and needs only to be set in place.

The resulting structure suggests a row of precise, fragile barracks, though I have no idea what purpose they're intended to serve. For now, I almost prefer not to know, amid the great relief they've brought; they seem like an act of pity someone has taken on me, for thanks to them, I can no longer see from my bedroom the doorway where Leila sometimes appears.

Towards nightfall the installation concludes. Narrow

signboards communicate that I now live in the vicinity of MUNICIPAL KIOSK NO. 20. And below it, Nos. 19 and 18, and above, Nos. 21, 22, and 23.

I begin to complete the requirements for my betrothal.

I make inquiries into the movements of the newly silent Besarión. At the company, the thread breaks off with his letter of resignation; at his apartment, with the removal of all the furniture.

With only the one signature on it, mine, I deposit the petition at City Hall. The city sends an inspector and an engineer. I ask them to listen. They tell me that noise falls under the purview of another office; they only handle construction issues.

They leave for a while to examine the wall from the other side.

They come back. They try to dissuade me from pursuing the complaint. The building is old, the wall unstable. If I have more bricks added to create an enclosure seven meters wide and two meters high, the municipality will determine that the weight is excessive and entrains a risk. They'll order that the wall be demolished and that a party wall as high as the one I'm requesting be built, though with shared expenses and a long period of inconvenience.

Still, I think I perceive that the engineer registers the nature of the problem quite intimately. I beg him for at least an idea.

He does me a favor, to the extent that he can. "I'll require a light enclosure, with vertical plywood slats. It won't do much for you, but..."

Later they put it in. And no, it doesn't do much for me.

*

I'm pleased to see a new look of satisfaction on my mother's face, one I will not deprive her of.

"I don't have to walk anymore. I step out to the sidewalk and find all the vegetables I need: fruit, milk, fresh eggs—even flowers!"

But these kiosks, the row of barracks, which are so useful to her, come to life before dawn.

Trucks, their engines hoarse and gasping, burst through the night into my sleep. They pull loudly into place and continue idling as their drivers prematurely predict buenos días, shout out quantities, and hurl boxes to the ground, bottles clanging within metal frames.

Vendors empty vegetables from crates then sent flying and crashing, some splintering apart; they hum obstinately, exchange explosive insults, chat with the newspaper delivery-man who pauses on the sidewalk in front of our house, or with some other colleague so far away that they have to shout. Women observe their ritual devotion to the broom: it scrapes, the hose hisses, boys show up with thermoses, their voices on the verge of manhood, to stroll by calling out "Café... caféééé..."

When my mother comes in with the breakfast mug, the vendors are insisting on prices that the earliest marketgoers vehemently dispute.

I know I am the subject of distressed and onerous conversations between Nina and my mother. But I didn't know how many.

"We have the house my father left us," Nina tells me. "It can be for us. Mamá has agreed."

Nina's new plural organizes in a very natural way the family to which she, myself, and my mother all belong.

"It's rented out," I say.

"Yes. But I talked to the lawyer. He suggests a swap. The renter and his wife come here, we go there."

She doesn't say, "The house my father left is better than this one." I understand: the house she inherited is not blighted by noise.

We let a week go by, for we imagine that only a Sunday can offer enough hours of leisure to explain this plan to the renter, persuade him, agree on the details of the swap, and, if necessary, write out the conditions.

Nina takes me there and introduces me. She's clever and uses our engagement to introduce the offer. I perceive that she plans to use it as a pretext for reclaiming the house, as well. But the renter is also astute.

"Well, well: congratulations, congratulations to you both. However, señorita, if you're planning to tell me that 'the newly wed want a home and a bed,' all I can tell you is that I'm married too, and my wife wants us to go on living in this home, which, I must respectfully remind you, your father was very happy to rent to us."

I intervene to explain the possibility of a swap.

"And where is your house . . . ?"

I tell him.

"That won't do, señor, that doesn't work for us, I can see that already. I've got my job here, just around the corner . . . and my wife is very fond of the neighbors."

I've noticed cracks on the wall next to the front door. Like the scratches a mop leaves on a floor, they're multiplying, and run almost all the way up the parlor's back wall. I transfer this information to my memory.

Besarión's mother is moved and surprised to see me. "The engineer...!" Charitably, I do not correct an impression that connects me to her boy. Her error has the unexpected benefit of causing the daughter to stop viewing me as unfit to come inside the house.

The señora is taking on the same joyless obesity as the sofa that she didn't ask to sit on. First, she inclines her head ruefully. She understands now that I've been thinking about her. Then I give her the transfusion: I manifest specific interest in her son, an interest which, I can easily imagine, others don't feel he merits.

She brings out some letters in tissue-thin envelopes bearing stamps with landscapes and heraldic fleurs-de-lis. She also has a little box, something like the packaging a sample of elegant soap might come in.

I listen to the letters. Their brevity seems at odds with the frowning eloquence of the man writing them. Nothing goes very deep, and only the occasional paragraph suggests some troubling ambiguity, or, to put it another way, the uncertainty in which he lives or that he has assumed as a mask.

During the day I take my meals at an automat across from Cluny.

In the moldy garden that is blackening the ruins, a young woman reads and meditates, peaceful as death itself. Through the bars an artist paints her portrait and titles it *Life*.

I've smiled at her and said, "There are five centuries between us."

And she has answered, "No. Only the width of the street."

The letters end. The mother sighs, but contentedly, as if to ask, "Isn't that admirable...?"

Then she remembers, she grows excited, she makes haste: she hasn't yet displayed everything. There's still the little box.

Her workworn fingers employ all the zealous care that handling fragile, venerable things demands to extract the miniature replica of Notre-Dame de Paris that her son has sent her from the Île de France.

My chronic state of tension makes me alert to every clue.

I discover a black line winding obliquely from the wall of my house to municipal fruit and vegetable kiosk No. 20, visible from my window. With every step that draws me closer, I enter what sounds like a social gathering, with music. Radio music.

The line draws power from the main cable and feeds it to an apparatus that stands among the varied golds of oranges and lemons.

I can't offer him a greeting. Though in fact he's now my closest neighbor, the first person, every morning, who could wish me a good day. But he's made his choice, and it's not one that promotes normal relations between us.

I step inside, formulate a plan. Before handing him the papers, I turn to face him. "Your permit is for selling fruits and vegetables, not for playing music in the street."

He reacts without violence. Turning up his palms, as if to say, "Here's my game," he points out, "They provided the connection. No one said not to play music."

"No one said not to. But I live here, and there's no way anyone has stated or authorized that I have to listen to your radio all day."

He gives in immediately. "Bueno. If it bothers you, we'll turn it off. There. That better?"

Dizzy with triumph, I'm sweating and feel as if my chest has burst through the ribbon that marks the finish line. Yes. Much better.

The food I ingest at lunch does not resign itself to its destiny. I ask for a tea and say, "I think I have indigestion."

My mother seems to know better. "No. It's your nerves," she tells me, and buries herself in her household tasks, leaving me alone with my nerves (or indigestion).

I can nap for half an hour and I must, or the boss and general manager are sure to find fault with everything I do. They don't understand, they say, how I can make such mistakes. In turn, I've given up trying to understand them. How can they fail to recognize that error is engendered in the very root of man's being . . . ?

I fell asleep, and a visceral dream me shook me. Something's moving, there outside . . . !

Oh. It's only the other invasion, by the radio that has started up its chatter again in my window.

Now I'm coming back to things. In a moment the upheaval will pass, the acute commotion in my chest will subside.

Because, in the end, what was it . . . ? Nothing. Only an individual who's discovered that this is how we live now, each doing whatever he feels like at that moment, in defiance of any lunatic who might pretend otherwise.

We'll get rid of the house.

We'll have a house where the walls aren't plastered with adobe, where rainwater doesn't leak into the bedrooms. The kitchen, its tiles gleaming in perfect rows and equipped with every modern device, will be a temptation rather than a punishment. The bedroom will be one thing, the room for accumulating (and writing) books will be another, separate thing.

Of course this will require a plan and good luck. And time.

Because first this house must be sold, and then the other one that our thoughts have sketched out must be found or built. Our advantage will consist in having some money of our own; if it's not enough, we'll arrange for a loan from a bank.

Since the consecration of what exists between myself and Nina is also underway, we develop successive steps. The first is to sell off this house, where the only current that circulates is noise. The second is to do the same with the furniture, taking only the most essential items to a boardinghouse. The third phase is the sweetest: with some of the money from the sale, Nina and I, now married, will travel, while my mind rests and recuperates.

My mother awaits us at the boardinghouse, which upon our return becomes our (transitory) base of operations. Then we choose, we buy, and our new life ensues.

The plan—whether it was devised by all three of us or

was mine alone and accepted by the other two—is born beautiful and strong. Its further development lies so fully within our powers that our diminutive consultation in the kitchen soon turns into a tender party, with the libation of a bottle of white wine, old and semisweet.

I can still perceive something of the mechanical din that pounds at our back wall, and of a litigation established in the air directly over our yard, or so it seems, between two rival songstresses, the first emanating from the radio in back of us, the other from the one in the kiosk out front. I pay no attention.

Perhaps our house's obvious modesty makes prospective owners dream of acquiring it on the cheap. In any case, I seem to be living out a kind of documentary film about anxiety. The anxiety of finding a roof.

Yet I learn from the tiny ads in the newspapers that purchase value is now based on the land itself rather than whatever was built there several decades ago when ideas about how to arrange space were very different. Those with the funds to buy do so for the price of the land. Because the buyers compete against each other, the sale should provide me with the tidy profit I'm hoping for.

For now, the only immediate outcome of tracking those ads is to turn me into a prolific buyer of periodicals. In one, I come across a photo of the lion tamer we dined with after the circus performance.

The tamer's mane is as untamed as ever, in all the dishevelment of bad nights to which no comb can offer a morning remedy. He's under double guard. The caption takes the side of the guards, employing bloodthirsty adjectives and calling him a terrorist.

I remember Besarión.

———

I take a wife.

Nina has agreed that we begin our journey in a region of the interior where people do gentle work by old-fashioned methods and tourists do not circulate.

Her only hesitation concerned our lodging.

I consulted the tourism bureau and was informed of several destinations with good hotels, establishments that justify their existence when, twice a month, ranchers and auctioneers congregate at cattle fairs.

I chose dates that did not coincide with the December cattle fairs.

The immensity of the plain invites disbelief in science and adherence to the deceptive evidence that the earth is a single, vast flat surface.

At one edge of the plain, the sun seems to tolerate the slow pace of the car that is carrying us along, seems to be telling us: There's no hurry, I won't set just yet, I'll light your way long enough for you to reach your destination.

To entertain us in the meantime, it plays at painting itself red, spilling the paint all around, even very far away.

The small town, built of red brick and fenced off in wire mesh, allows itself to be invaded—by the little car—without alarm.

I take Nina's hand, which is gripping the seat, and give it a loving squeeze to transmit the great calm she has brought me, in anticipation of the peace that awaits us.

We step out, and our suitcases are taken down, to remain there with us for the ten days.

The little car's motor shuts off and my ears can now fully adjust to the atmosphere.

Something is audible. A powerful something.

A majestic pounding of iron against iron. A propagation of sound waves like layers of metal being tortured in the air until they escape across the grasslands.

It's the blacksmith. My childhood self identifies it; my adult self incorporates it into the logical framework of the primal village.

Forge and bellows, the anvil and its hammers . . . I'm inconsolable.

2

Nina and I were nomads for three years, and my mother, with her piano, for somewhat less than that.

Then we settled down. That lasted seventeen months, as attested by the number of receipts I possess for payment of rent.

Now we've moved into our house, which is something like the one we wanted.

———

The pedals fell off the piano, and this damage, though repairable, of course, worried my mother as an ill omen for the instrument.

The boardinghouse room was up a staircase with fourteen steps, a narrow staircase. As we were arranging for the move, I told my mother, "I don't think it will be possible to get the piano up there." My mother answered, "Well, hijo, then it won't be possible to get me up there." Consequently, that pension would not be our third residence. Instead we went to a different one on the ground floor, with easy access through wide double doors.

The piano let itself be hauled along. It was the largest, heaviest item in the succession of moving trucks that took us on our piecemeal tour of the city.

It reduced our living space. Here we ceded a parlor to it; there, a hallway. Special vigilance was always required to protect it from mistreatment by children, and on one occasion it generated an incomprehensible dispute. But the piano wasn't a matter of blind obstinacy on my mother's part. She needed it with her as a monument to the family's memories. For memories, as everyone knows, cannot be erased.

The dispute—which led to our departure from that boardinghouse—happened because the landlady's daughter was practicing her Chopin, without success, above my room. I didn't ask for much, only for something like mercy, but the landlady called me cruel and absurd, wept, and pointed at my piano, claiming that not only had I sacrificed that one but I wanted to sacrifice all other pianos too.

Her denunciation was unfair. Our piano made no sound only because we didn't know how to play it.

After the pedals were damaged, my mother again spoke of herself and the piano as inseparable. "We've come this far, hijo, but we can't follow you any farther."

She and the piano went to my uncle's house, and it did them good. Now that they've come back to live with us, my mother is sensible and resigned, and the instrument, silent as ever, maintains its discreet integrity and is protected from future risks and disruptions.

My mother's troubles were ours, as well. But it was in her blood to live where she could say "This is my house," or "This belonged to my parents and two previous generations with my name." I think she confused the boardinghouses with asylums or hospitals, or abandoned buildings full of squatters.

It was her opinion that at the very least we should rent a whole house for ourselves. I kept this desire of hers in check by arguing, "What for, when we'll soon be buying one ... ?"

In truth, and confidentially, the numbers were holding me back. We sold our house for nine hundred thousand pesos. The broker and the notary fees, along with the wedding expenses (clothing, reception, travel), brought that total down to eight hundred twenty thousand. We nibbled away at that eight hundred twenty, and then at the eight hundred that was left, and then the seven hundred eighty. The boardinghouse for the three of us (and the piano, which made bargaining harder) cost eighteen thousand, and later twenty-one, twenty-four, thirty, always more. Faced with these outlays, my salary lost its initial advantage over our expenses, became an even match for them, then yielded the lead.

In order to rent a whole house, we'd have to take a big bite out of our seven hundred eighty or seven hundred fifty thousand for key money, which would reduce the capital we had in hand for a purchase or construction.

At that point she would reiterate her complaint. "We should have bought that one ..."

That one: the house we liked better than any of the others. But my mother was forgetting.

"Mamá, you're forgetting. It was a Saturday. When we went back Monday we heard the noise from the sawmill behind it."

"Yes, and that made you wary. After that, you'd always spend some time nosing around the neighborhood."

"I believe that's how it's done."

If we were shown a house we liked, I would wander away from the conversation, leaving the seller with Nina or my mother while I went in search of noises that might filter in through walls or courtyards. This method generally resulted in unpleasantness. But if I stayed back and confessed my concern, the seller would think I was deliberately disparaging the property and ensnare me in useless discussions of the actual volume of this or that noise, or possible remedies for it.

Accordingly, when a house was for sale, if it interested us at all, I would make a tour of the neighborhood before going in. A sign in the street behind or off to one side might reveal the block's noisy interstices: PLASTER FACTORY, STOVE FACTORY, METAL STRUCTURES, MARBLE WORKS, WHOLESALE HARDWARE ... Grinding machines, roaring ovens, shuddering motors, gigantic rivets, the loading and unloading of metal plates, the inexhaustibly patient saws used for slicing up blocks of marble. Or else, even closer, the smaller workshops: AUTO-BODY REPAIR, VULCANIZING, ENDLESS SAWS SHARPENED.

Endless.

"There was also the merry-go-round ..."

"Right, of course. With the loudspeaker that would start wheezing through its repertoire of tunes in the morning and keep it up all day."

"But," Nina expressed a reservation, "the merry-go-round didn't stop us from buying anything ..."

"That's true, it only sent us running from another boardinghouse, the fifth or sixth one."

"The fourth. The fifth had the nightclub hidden away in the basement."

"No, that was the sixth. The fifth overlooked the pub ..."

"...with little tables on the sidewalk, and at night, under our balcony, arguments, singing, gossip, transistor radios, waiters taking orders, forks falling, glasses shattering…"

"The motorcycles standing next to the stone wall with their engines running, their defiant riders in black jackets accelerating from a dead stop…"

"The parking attendants' whistles…"

"The drag racers, who always chose that block.… Getting ready for the race, brakes squealing, fistfights… Burning rubber at the starting line, motors backfiring…"

We've fallen silent, steeped in our memories of the clamorous uproar that continually assailed our place of repose when we tried to sleep. Until Nina acknowledges, "Yes, it was the fifth one. Or the seventh, I can't remember. An odd number."

"It's all the same. Already by then our money was no good."

Nine hundred thousand they gave us. And seven hundred eighty, seven hundred fifty, or seven hundred thousand would have afforded us a certain prudent purchase power. But our resources stagnated, then diminished, and within two years we'd have needed one million eight hundred thousand, for a house that suited us.

The roof.

The noise is a set of bongo drums.

The beat brings on a state of more-noise and wards off those addicted to no-noise.

It's part of the aggression "against Father, against the Man."

(Disdain is the most benign and indulgent form of this hostility.)

"Get in the noise." That's the slogan. They've made their

choice, and for a reason. Noise has become the sign or symbol of all that is now, all that is new, all that possesses weight and validity: the rupture.

"The world will belong to the noise or will not be." "Silence is for the dead." Yes...

The bongos are an emanation, an armature, a combative rejection, or the lead-up to a combat that will never take place against the *whole* of the enemy, visible or not. (The drummer pounding the bongos thinks only of himself.)

The recorded children's chorus continually broadcast by the merry-go-round's loudspeaker demanded that I make up for an omission. "If at least having it so close by could provide some fun for a child of ours..."

Nina stiffened, as if at the mention of a secret sorrow. She refused me. "Yes, a child of our own. A child who can take over for the piano in the moving vans."

I let myself vanish into my silence and my cigarette's peaceful smoke. She said nothing more. Later she calmed down.

I bore a wound inflicted by children. A real wound.

At our boardinghouse, a pink wrought-iron gate—wide slats with rosettes below and thick, contoured bars ending in spear tips above—looked like a good potential subject for the rotogravure page of a newspaper.

At the same time, it protected the garden, the one thing that softened the prisonlike aspect of our room.

Some urchins came up with the idea of throwing stones at it. The whole band of them welcomed the initiative and every night after sunset the gate endured their disgraceful bombardment.

Those clattering stones fell inside my head. The vein developed a suspicious fear of them and would begin palpitating at the very thought of the volley.

I defended the gate, chased the kids away.

One evening I found the group clustered quietly on the ground. I took my papers up to the room, then came back down to the garden, suspecting them of having some renewed attack in mind. Stubbornly intent on doing nothing, they didn't glance my way.

I leaned against the gate in a show of ownership. That seems to have been what they were waiting for. Erupting from the ground, they all hurled pieces of rubble like grenades. Four, five—many!—hit me in the face.

People started giving me looks after that, and we emigrated to another neighborhood.

Nina's attachment had declined. She took care of me, protected me, but did she respect me as before? Perhaps not.

We left another boardinghouse because of the landlady's record player. Nina usually managed to be sure it was switched off by the time I came home from work, or that the volume was turned down, at least.

One day she didn't have time to go and plead with the landlady. The blaring music went straight to my head and I invaded the kitchen demanding explanations. I shouted.

The landlady shouted back. "¡Qué tanto...! What's all the fuss? Silence, always silence when the señor is home. And when he's not, the one playing records is his wife."

Reflecting on this later, I told myself that I am no enemy of music, nor is my wife, nor have I asked her to be.

But the landlady was already demanding that we leave.

I thought that when we had a home, a home of our own, without noise, Nina's small doubts about me would be set straight.

*

Someone (not Besarión, not me) is full of love for everyone.

Someone (not Besarión, not me) is full of hatred for everyone.

Someone is full of reservations, mistrust, and suspicion of everyone. (It may be Besarión, it may be me.)

Someone is full of violence towards everyone. (Each one of us is, everyone is.)

Someone needs to be respected and loved. (That's me, that's Besarión.)

But is it truly possible for anyone to be full of love for everyone?

I came to learn that Schopenhauer was on my side. "If you cut up a large diamond into little bits, it will entirely lose the value it had as a whole; and an army divided up into small bodies of soldiers loses all its strength. So a great intellect sinks to the level of an ordinary one, as soon as it is interrupted and disturbed . . . for its superiority depends upon its power of concentration—of bringing all its strength to bear upon one theme, in the same way as a concave mirror collects into one point all the rays of light that strike upon it.

"Therefore, eminent spirits—Kant, Goethe, Lichtenberg, Jean-Paul—have always shown an extreme dislike to disturbance in any form . . . Above all have they been averse to that violent interruption that comes from noise. Ordinary people are not much put out by anything of the sort."

Reading this page produced a melancholy state of mind, for while it placed me among the ranks of those who can be interrupted and disturbed, thus offering one possible motive for the reiterated postponement of my book—which I generally attributed to the instability of my housing situation—it also caused me to note the absence of an effective check or balance for noise in my own case, since I can't claim to possess an eminent spirit.

Schopenhauer, and his "Noise is a torture to intellectual people...": "The most inexcusable and disgraceful of all noises is the cracking of whips—a truly infernal thing when it is done in the narrow resounding streets of a town."

I smiled.

It occurred to me to share my discovery with Reato, the journalist. I went to his newspaper to take him this clarifying, fulminating article.

He published it in two columns under the following terse and striking headline:

WHIP-CRACKING

He added in a fantasy of his own about Schopenhauer in the second half of the twentieth century. Besieged by the noise of the mechanized city, the eminent German philosopher suffers an initial convulsion of bewilderment and strong desire to flee into the past, then arms himself with a coachman's whip, precisely the kind he used to hate, and goes forth to punish guilty parties and machines.

Reato was praised for this publication. He asked me to bring him other suggestions of the same sort.

None of the others were ever as successful, but the series,

which benefited greatly from my contributions, eventually won him a seat on the city council.

I would bring him a clipping, usually some news item. He'd copy it and give it a headline. At most, he might bestir himself to make some comparison, as pretext for an additional brief comment of his own, a redundant observation or bit of acid criticism. Then he'd sign it (with his name).

DOUCEMENT...

Final scenes of a French film:

Daylight dawns in a city intersected by a river. Two fishermen step out of an alley and walk toward the quay. Alert and content (it's a Sunday), they whistle a tune.

A policeman in a blue cape points to the nearby buildings where people are still asleep, puts a finger to his lips, and councils, "Doucement..."

The film ends without sound. The camera pans across the Seine, all the dwellings in deep repose. The word Fin appears, in silence.

THE POUNDING HEART

The decibel is a measure of the relative intensity of sound.

An ordinary automotive-repair shop produces noise in the range of 80 to 100 decibels. An orchestra playing fortissimo can reach 110. The riveting of steel plates, 120.

Up to this level, sound is tolerable to human ears.

Beyond it comes the pain threshold.

Above 70 decibels, the physiological reaction begins. The heart pounds desperately, the skin and other organs grow numb and rigid.

You, a hardy, heedless citizen, assure me that it doesn't bother you. You don't know; you'll become aware of the effect only when it's almost too late.

In one neighborhood of New York City, the local children's physical and intellectual development is delayed by the noise from demolitions. This has been scientifically proven and reported by Professor Trémelières of the Academy of Medicine in Paris.

Sick people who receive care in a noisy environment suffer more complications (Trémelières).

Meanwhile, the Max Planck Institute for the Physiology of Work in Dortmund, West Germany, is performing a series of experiments in soundproof booths and finding that the impact of noise on blood circulation, auditory capacity, and the dilation of the pupils varies from person to person.

The institute is developing methods that muffle sound at its origin or protect the human organism by other appropriate means.

THUNDER (AND MEN) AGAINST NOISE

MUNICH—Thunder is used to combat noise at the Technical University's High Voltage Laboratory. A bolt of lightning unleashes an artificial storm in a Faraday cage. The noise level is measured inside an experimental building constructed of newly developed materials. Despite the ultrahigh volume, 98 percent of the sound is absorbed by the masonry.

MADRID—Everyone may one day possess his own "noise deflector." Preuss (engineer, age 42) has researched methods for keeping soundwaves from expanding towards the earth. If his ideas are adopted, supersonic jets will no longer break windows or eardrums with their shock waves. The device will have an infinitude of applications, including a personal "deflector" for each person.

LONDON—The future belongs to the deaf. Young people listen to music at high volume, which affects their hearing. Within a few years, their generation may suffer from deafness. A simple mechanism can alleviate the problem. It disconnects the record player automatically when a certain volume is exceeded.

INTERMEZZO
Phoenician Tale
from the
Pre-Christian Era

A poet lives between a blacksmith and a boilermaker.

A martyr to noise, he pays them both to move away.

They accept his offer and keep the agreement: the boilermaker moves into the blacksmith's house and the blacksmith moves into the boilermaker's.

FRANKFURT—After the electric car comes the electric omnibus, already in service. Elimination of economic dependence on petroleum. Less pollution in cities. Promise of an almost silent, more humane public transit.

LONDON—Stifle it at the source. A question for the undersecretary of transportation. He reveals an agreement with the manufacturers of motorcycles, which henceforth will be equipped with a mechanism that muffles or eliminates their noise.

WATFORD, U.K.—All sound from the outside kept at bay. An invention of the British Building Research Establishment: a hydraulic window, connected to a sensor with a microphone. It closes automatically. Ideal for those living in the vicinity of airports and highways.

PARIS, NEW YORK, BONN, etc.—Associations (and Mayors, and City Councils) against Noise. In Santiago, Chile, one such association was founded by a journalist, Arriagada.

Our scientific and technological researchers, doctors, sanitation experts, legislators, city councilmen, architects, urbanists, judges, and policemen neither seek to ward it off, nor defend us against it, nor prepare to defend us in the future. This must be a matter of vision: some lack insight, others turn a blind eye.

The intermezzo constituted one of Reato's few personal contributions. Another was to occasionally rework—sometimes in a jocular or festive tone, rarely with any ingenuity—the items, taken from daily papers and magazines, that I provided him with.

His little Phoenician tale didn't contribute much to the point, but I heard it repeated as casual chitchat, which probably means it caught on with readers more than the serious examples did.

I drew his attention to this contradiction and Reato tried to defend himself with crafty flattery. "I put it in to demonstrate that noise has been a problem for thousands of years, and someone has always had to confront it, some sensible, enlightened man such as yourself, or, in all modesty, myself."

I smiled at him indulgently and asked where he'd run across the tale. He said he'd read that it was carved on some Phoenician ruin; in his opinion some Ionesco of antiquity must have come up with it.

That was Reato.

He didn't go so far as to establish a chimerical antinoise association in imitation of the one founded by his praiseworthy though entirely fictional colleague in Santiago, but when it came to his own personal benefit, he went much farther.

He drafted—with my help—a noise-nuisance ordinance that didn't elicit much of a reaction from the city council, but that did attract readers who felt themselves to be understood and communicated their gratitude to him in various ways.

The leaders of a political party took note of the journalist's popularity and thought to turn it to their advantage. They listed Reato as a candidate and he won more votes than the professional politicians. I don't think this was entirely due to support for his campaign against noise; having grown used to seeing his name in the paper, people were confident he could solve all kinds of local problems.

Once on the city council, he pushed our draft law forward, and the city finally had its lyrical ordinance, while Reato had the concrete benefits of his office. He held the seat for two years and never again evinced the slightest concern about noise or anything else of any importance.

And no one else evinced the slightest concern about him. He was over.

He believed himself to be securely and profitably set up in his new position, and once he had ascended to it, his interest in the news items I'd discovered and furnished for his column dwindled. Several went unused, though to my mind they were every bit as worthy of a box of their own as his intermezzo.

This one, for example, with a moral that could be described as "Ultracivilized whites should heed this example," which was taken from the Dogon people, black, indigenous to Africa, and culturally quite primitive, who were observed by anthropologists during a rigorously contemporary moment: our own.

```
  Silence, in fact, for the Dogon peo-
ple, when not born of fear, is a much-
appreciated social quality.

  (From the Esposti-Andreitti Report on
Africa)
```

Besarión was working at an international travel agency.

He told me he applied for the job on the basis of his own experience as a traveler, yet he surmised that the manager had hired him because of qualities suggested by his surname, which Besarión translated for him as el caminante, the walker.

I asked how he was living. He answered, "Alone."

"Solitude emancipates," I said.

"Solitude is impossible," he turned and said back to me.

I thought about the cramped life of boardinghouses, the alien ideas that distract us from insomnia's profound individuality, and said to myself: He's right. Solitude is impossible.

But he had spoken the phrase merely to introduce a practical proposal: he was inviting me to share a house and the cost of its rental.

He'd bring his mother, I'd bring mine.

I imagined a symmetrical house: on one side of the hallway, my room, then my mother's; on the other side, Besarión's, then his mother's.

I conveyed the news: "I'm married." Which destroyed any such parallelism. "I know," he said.

I asked how much we'd each pay. He told me. I imagined he must have made some mistake, since the total monthly expense was an amount I could easily afford on my own. He seemed to be quite certain, however, and I didn't want to argue.

"Where is this house?"

He told me.

He didn't come back. I went looking for him, but he wasn't working there anymore.

Later I learned that his mother had died. Not before the proposal that we all live together, but afterward.

I looked for the house and it wasn't some dream Besarión had dreamt.

In the entryway, a fellow just past middle age was sweeping the mosaic floor.

"Is the house unoccupied?"

"Since yesterday."

"It's for rent?"

He laid aside the broom and came closer to peer into my face.

"How do you know? Did someone send you?"

"Besarión."

"Besarión. Is that a name?"

The fellow just past middle age was the owner, and he belonged to an identifiable species: the good man.

We walked through the yard. It used to be continuous with the one next door. The low wall that ran down the middle between them didn't contradict an impression of unity and communication.

"It's empty," I observed, looking at the house on the other side.

"And will stay that way."

"Much longer?"

"Who knows? Probably a lot longer."

"Why?"

For some reason, the State had appropriated the house. And quite plausibly, the State had forgotten all about it, the record of ownership misfiled somewhere in some inventory of State holdings.

We moved over the course of a Saturday and Sunday. I recovered my box of books. The vermin were astonishingly persistent, but the books had somehow survived.

I still needed Monday morning, and stole those hours from work at the company.

When I came home that evening, Nina told me, "I'm glad you're home early. I was scared."

"Scared? Of what?"

"The solitude, all the silence…"

Another time I got back very late. Nina was asleep and dinner was laid out for me in the kitchen. I ate it all and remained in my chair, immersed in the night's untroubled flow. I was alone the way a person is alone in the shower. I drank the wine, savoring it as if it were more than an ordinary vintage.

I began constructing paragraphs of *The Roof*; the time had come to write the book. That was my task for the next day, the following evening, Sunday, the upcoming holiday… I don't know. Meanwhile, I would repeat the first distinct sentences of the work to myself. They lived up to all my hopes.

In reality I resisted giving myself over to the book. Soon I was hard at work getting it to slip through the cracks.

———

The adjacent house was reopened. The government had remembered it and was arranging to put a police station there. For now, carpenters and painters were laboring to make it somewhat presentable.

I accepted the prospect of shadowy troop movements—preparations for nocturnal raids—as well as the last blusterings of drunks picked up from the town square, and the shouts of squabbling sisters-in-law whose quarrel would continue even as the officer wrote them both up. Yet none of that dismayed me. Instead, I was confident that the stable presence of the police would promote a general restraint, throughout the neighborhood or even just on our block.

It must not be supposed that miscreants forsake their audacity and allow themselves to be arrested so regularly as to provide continual activity for those on duty in police stations. Or at least that wasn't how things went at the station next door to me. And as a distraction during the tedious shift that ran from nine p.m. until dawn, the officers brought in a radio.

The noise-nuisance ordinance is very clear on this point: complaints regarding nocturnal violations of its stipulations must be registered at the nearest police station.

The ordinance I myself contributed to putting in place, that is. With insufficient foresight, I'd come to realize.

You can sleep while hearing a radio, that's true, but you have to get ready for it. You have to court sleep, wear yourself out, drink too much during dinner, not speak much at night, not excite yourself.

At the company, the boss would say, "Excuse me, is this work terribly fatiguing for you?"

And I had to explain. "What I'm doing is preparing myself to sleep."

Once he wanted to know more. "And how do you do that?"

"Just as I'm doing: by letting myself be, half-asleep, my eyelids lowered, trying to lose all awareness."

"And this preparation, it must begin at the office?"

It's the year 1830 and we—my men and I—are stationed on the consequential plain, battling over the nation's future.

I'm the one with the most to lose sleep over: I must foresee, I must plan, I must remain on the alert. I have to fight, too, like all the others, but on the front lines.

The enemy's movements are cunning and mysterious. I believe they have us surrounded, though no attack reveals their full force.

Thirty men fall upon us. We shoot, slit throats, put spears into ten. Later come thirty more, or thirty-five.

Nor can I see their caudillo: he leads from the rear. Perhaps holding himself in reserve.

Sleeping becomes a thorny problem, especially now; the scavenging animals have grown bolder and make no distinction between the living and the dead.

Each time I try to sleep, our attackers, the Montoneras, come back.

I'm the commander, I think, but I'll be overcome with sleep and they'll destroy us.

Rapid blinking defends me a while longer. The restorative effect of maté is intense but fleeting.

"Mi comandante." A rasping, velvety voice, a black man's voice, calls me back.

One day very soon I won't hear him. And he'll see the maté and my hand, still gripping it tightly.

After dinner Nina brought me a soothing maté with linden flowers.

Some nights she'd try to scribble her police bulletins into my ears, telling me, for example, "They brought in the girl, the one who killed her fiancé. She'll kill herself, too. She was screaming for them to give her a gun."

A single gesture dammed the flow. "Don't give me thoughts. Thoughts will keep me from sleeping."

To tell the truth, she no longer had much to say to me. She'd wrap herself up in her song, her soft little song. She was singing to the child growing inside her.

Except for such moments of strain, we lived like everyone else.

We'd go to the movies, see family, visit the homes of certain married couples and invite them, in turn, to our dining room, or join them on short expeditions in their cars. We were not strangers to restaurants, picnics in the park, parades.

From time to time, like everyone else, we laughed.

Like everyone else, we had a television set, though like very few people, we used it with discretion.

"No one's throwing me out of here."

Then he changed his tune. "They'll throw me out of here when I'm dead!"

And finally, he headed death off in a different direction. "If they throw me out of here, I'll kill him."

It was me he was going to kill.

Because it was me who persuaded Nina to stop recognizing him as our tenant and stop accepting his money, a tactic he countered—not without considerable effort—first by directly depositing the rent in our bank, and later by depositing it with the courts.

Then I exhibited his cracks (the cracks in the walls of the house) and argued that the municipality could not vouch for the safety of such dangerous walls.

I put this in writing. And did not place my trust in the

eloquence of my missive alone, but paid a visit to the commissioner of the Buildings Department. The commissioner was my former geometry professor, whose professional rectitude, especially when it came to flunking students, always proved strikingly mathematical.

My former professor waxed paternal and reminisced. I confided I needed the house to save me from the police station's radio. He mentioned a certain business and the name of a commercial product. That was how I became acquainted with wax plugs, which come lightly swaddled in cotton and mold to the shape of our ear canals.

When I began using them, my wristwatch surprised me. I checked the time, and it was no longer manifesting a busy ticking as it had before. I blamed myself for not having wound it, but quickly noticed the movement of the thin second hand.

The plugs reduced my auditory capacity just enough that—there, right next to the police station—the radio's ordinary volume became a tolerable murmur.

One night I dreamed witches were whispering in a corner of the ceiling.

By day, I thought that even in my dreams I lacked all talent or ambition for heroism. I never once compared myself to Ulysses, though he also stopped his ears with wax so as not to hear the sirens' treacherous song.

Nina's little song was also erased, because I used the plugs by day as well. She had to raise her voice to get through to me. If she forgot, I had to ask "What?" repeatedly until she'd realize and speak louder.

Sometimes she spoke as if waging war against deafness, and I'd gaze at her calmly, wait for her to finish what she was saying, and explain, "You don't need to shout, I'm not using the plugs." These moments of confusion did not delight us. Sometimes she burst into tears. I asked why. She replied, "It's ridiculous."

"Everything? That I do?"

"I don't know. I don't judge you. But when I feel like I'm being ridiculed, which I do right now, you should allow me to let it out, at least."

"By crying?"

I wondered why I didn't know how to offer consolation.

Do you know? Have you thought about it?

The darkness was silence.

Silence preceded the Creation.

Silence was the uncreated, and we, the created, emerged from silence.

Can sound gain access to the maternal womb?

Had my organs of hearing not yet developed, and that's why I can find no trace or memory of any sound there?

From silence were we made, and to the dust of silence shall we return.

Someone begs, "That I may recover the peace of former nights . . ." And is given a vast silence, utterly serene, without boundaries. (At the cost of his life.)

Our nights, Nina, lack compassion. And soul.

My former professor sent for me. He read me the inspector's report, which was unfavorable to my aims.

"The inspector is a friend of the tenant," he said. "I know that. But I'm a friend of yours. Or don't you know that?"

It was after learning that the report ran counter to his

interests that the tenant began verbally invoking my death. In the end, he would be not the last unfortunate soul to do so.

He went to see my lawyer. My lawyer phoned me with advice. "Give him something, and he'll quit scheming and leave."

I said, "Good."

"How much do you think?"

"I have—my mother and I have—two hundred and thirty-four thousand pesos. Since the house will be for her too, we can do without half of it, if necessary."

"Is that all you've got? Don't give him that much."

"Why not?"

"Because you have to pay my fee, too."

There were papers to sign, with specifics on the moving date, indemnification, renunciation of rights, and so on. Nina signed as the owner. As her spouse, I placed my signature beneath hers.

The tenant was there with us.

"Where will you go?" I asked.

"I'll buy a house. I sold a piece of land, I have some savings, and what you're giving helps"—his smile was mordant—"even if it only covers the moving expenses. But I'll have to look for a house and I don't have anything in mind right now. Meanwhile, we'll go to a boardinghouse."

A boardinghouse. A roof. A movable roof.

I thought of actions one carries out even though they run counter to one's sense of charitable virtue.

Nina, that time, thought I was a good man. She told me so.

———

We sell Nina's house and buy another, one without a past.

When I take my mother there, she says, "That's strange . . . If I told you, you wouldn't believe me."

"What?"

"Last night I dreamed about this house."

It wasn't last night.

The neighborhood is inoffensive.

Nothing bothers me here except one local idiot. He dresses like a mechanic (which he is) and doesn't annoy anyone when he's busy at his garage, which is off somewhere else. But when he hangs around here on his days off, his preference is for the street and his gang on the corner. He grows guttural and imitates monkeys and other animals. This appears to be a tactic to keep the group from excluding him. When he's all by himself, he takes a stone and bangs it against the hollow pole of a streetlamp. He hits it, then puts his ear against the metal column and listens. When the vibration comes to an end, he hits again.

He lives in the boardinghouse across the street, the one with three courtyards. I believe he's the landlady's son.

I consider man a maker of noises.

His noises are different from the noises of the cosmos or those of nature.

Man is a natural emitter of sounds: his voice (speech, song). He also uses tools to produce sound: a rock or piece of iron struck against something; the various methods of making music, machines . . . (Noise machines.)

Machines are useful. Their noise is not, and still less so

when amplified or uncontrolled. At present, machine noise is neither moderated nor controlled nor suppressed. It produces the euphoria of power in those who generate it. (Aggressive power?)

Human beings are generators of sound. Other people are sonority itself.

I'd have to shun the proximity of all people. And that isn't my attitude. In fact, I'm quite trusting.

There is a kind of noise that is … material.

And another kind that is … what is it?

It comes from people themselves, the conditions people create, coexistence.

Sometimes it comes as a wall, or a wave, or an infiltration of sound, or as a whisper that's both oppressive and depressing.

Actually it's not like that at all. It cannot be heard. These characteristics—you have to imagine them, intuit them. The part of it that can be grasped, that is received, are the consequences. Essentially—like the other kind, the material kind of noise—it disturbs. Its gravitation is so intense that it destabilizes not the senses … but what … ?

Is it even a noise … ? Yes, it must constitute a noise: a war noise, destructive though not apparent. An instrument of not-allowing-to-be.

(I digress. I fear this line of reasoning has been a blast of unreason.)

My house isn't deep, it soon comes to an end. Better. If it extended into the heart of the block, an auto-repair shop might one day reach it, or a factory of some sort.

My little room for being alone sits at the top of the building—an unintended tower. I've lined it with books. I await their renewed contagion. What I have within me requires their slow infiltration. It will revive.

Perhaps I shouldn't make *The Roof* (or whatever it ends up being called) my apprenticeship, but save it for my more mature period.

I could begin with a novel that demanded less responsibility, to exercise my style, activate my imagination. A crime novel?

Sabotaging certain formulas of the crime novel. Generally, the author of such a work knows who the murderer is but hides that from the police and the reader until the end, tossing in red herrings to throw everyone off.

My novel will have a crime and various suspects, but I myself, the author, will remain unaware of who the criminal is. That way the book can be prolonged indefinitely, until the crime it once was about has been entirely forgotten.

Or it could have one of the following endings: (a) readers may select the murderer at will, on the basis of whatever motives and evidence strike them as most convincing, which is to say that for every reader who reaches a conclusion, the criminal could be a different character; or (b) some random event or canny policeman—an event or a policeman within the story—reveals the criminal, and that's how both reader and author learn who it is.

Another possibility occurs to me: the policeman discovers the identity of the evildoer but doesn't yet have him in custody. He notifies the police chief by phone that the investigation is complete and he's on his way to see him—the chief—and reveal the murderer's identity. He hangs up, visibly upset. He drives recklessly, has an accident, dies. Since the criminal's name was only in the policeman's mind and remained unspoken, the chief never learns it and neither does the author.

An equally admissible thesis is that the criminal has described his own crime but out of sheer mental confusion fails to recognize himself as a criminal, believing himself to be no more than a writer.

But I have no experience writing a crime novel either. If I decide to write one before proceeding to *The Roof*, I'll have to choose a subject, within reality, as a possible victim, and imagine myself as the killer. That way, studying the other, studying myself, I can gradually build up the book.

Maybe the monkey could be the victim.

If the monkey bothers me, it's because I can hear him. If I can hear the monkey and his banging on lampposts and his gang on the corner, it's because my bedroom gives, via its balcony, onto the street.

If, just now, the sound of a radio under the window is making my nerves jump, it's because the Avenida de Acceso runs by, two hundred meters away, and truck drivers turn off its rapid flow of traffic to find a spot on a quiet street. They park behind a house, eat in the shade, sleep on cots in the truck's cabin, don their best clothes, and treat the city as a port of call. The trucks have radios.

From the balcony, I dispute their right to their radios and to camp out among peoples' homes.

But they lose nothing if this street is barred to them, and in their certainty of never seeing me again after today or tomorrow, they can always outdo me. I feel my stomach churning into a red ball of indignation, like my face.

I start to think that they—and not, for the moment, the monkey—would be the most suitable victims. I would make the bodies vanish completely, and the trucks, without drivers, without visible owners, would stand there below my balcony, motionless and vanquished for weeks on end with the sun beating down on them, like tanks abandoned in the desert whose occupants have dispersed across the sands.

———

The tides bring Besarión back to me.

"What seas were you lurking under?"

"I was on a trip."

"Again?"

"Again. I was in Switzerland. I was called."

He accepted the invitation, he tells me, with some hesitation; he didn't speak the language of the Germanic region.

"The invitation came from Ludwig Lücke, a name easy to remember but hard to fathom. I was given a hotel on the Sihlstrasse in Zurich. There, I found my mailbox stuffed with itineraries and programs, train tickets and invitations."

"At no cost to you . . . ?"

"At no cost to me. In the Stadttheater I saw *Lohengrin* and *Orpheus in der Unterwelt*, in the Schauspielhaus, *König Lear*. On a mountainside, a whole town put on *Wilhelm Tell* in front of a cabin. I delved into the vestiges of Lucerne's past: the giant's kettles left by glaciers; the bridge covered by a chapel with triangular paintings, remote and mystical. I stood before three decapitated angels who bore in their hands their own heads, eyelids closed: the patron saints of Zurich, in the *collégiale*."

"Anything any less serious?"

"Yes, a reception at the Rathaus. Formal attire required. Ludwig Lücke hadn't anticipated the meager contents of my suitcase. I rented a tuxedo and went to the Rathaus, an eighteenth-century baroque structure on a pier. I danced, drank marc (a kind of grappa), made friends. Suddenly (while eating white sausages served with mustard long after dinner) I wondered: Shouldn't Ludwig Lücke be here? If this is a celebration hosted by the State, and he's an important figure, I should be able to locate him among all the tuxedos. I asked. Everyone knew who he was, but no one seemed able to identify him.

"Then I sat down and said to myself: I don't know who he is, but Ludwig Lücke is able to provide me with things all along the route he laid out for me. Where was he when I couldn't manage to get anything for myself? Where will he be after this journey, when I need him?"

He allows himself a moment, which I respect. Then I intervene.

"Besarión, what are you looking for now?"

He answers, perhaps only to himself, "The sign, the signal."

I can't ask what the signal is. He won't let me. I change the subject. "Was Ludwig Lücke of any use in helping you find it?"

"No. I never saw him. I did learn some German words. *Lücke* means emptiness."

The monkey has left me no time for my literary exercise. I still haven't planned out how to do away with him and he's already decamping, along with his mother's whole establishment, which is moving out of the house with three courtyards.

At least this spares me the guttural noises produced by the landlady's son.

*

I relate the second voyage of my friend Besarión to Nina and my mother.

I expurgate all that is least credible from the narrative. Nevertheless, my mother says, "I've seen him going door-to-door. He was trying to sell a set of used cutlery. He had it wrapped in newspaper. He'd open the package to show the bundles of knives and spoons."

Besarión tries to be, pretends to be, but only so as not to be. Not to be what? Not to be who? Himself. Besarión decidedly tends not to be.

As for me, do I tend not to be . . . ? No: I tend to be. But I'm not allowed to; I'm interfered with, blocked. I can be only under certain conditions. What conditions I don't know. I have only the vaguest sense of them.

Such as the condition of being here with myself. Is this solitude? Perhaps it might be called profound solitude.

Though if I'm here with myself, I'm accompanied. Since I'm here with myself, I'm not alone: there are two of us. "To be with" means "together with someone or something else," not the same one or thing.

If there are two of us, we constitute one and the other. Which is me? I say: I myself and the one who's here with me. Then, the one who's here with me is the other. Or if I say "to be with myself" do I thereby suppose an "I myself" and another "I myself"?

I should have said "to be here in myself" and then my thoughts wouldn't have gotten so tangled up.

It's all been a way of abandoning myself to the seduction of words. Ideas that are the properties or features of words seem to unveil something to you, as if alerting you to the nature of their deepest layers. They started to confound me, and a fear began taking shape within me: a fear of being two, of harboring another, of having lost my other self or of finding myself under its dominion.

Now I'm getting entangled once more, but that's because I've again said something that inescapably disturbs me: to be within myself. Why did I say that?

I'd established the need for certain conditions in order to be, such as the condition of "being with myself," which I then changed to "being in myself." And now I fear the meaning of the second phrase may be the same as the first's. "In" suggests that I'm within the interior of the other. The sum of that, once again, is two.

"To be beside oneself" is also something people say... So-and-so was beside himself, I'm beside myself, etc. These are very common, graphic expressions that have nothing to do with the condition of being. Which reveals how absurd this argument with myself is.

"Beside oneself" refers to breaking out of the social and conventional mold one adopts, and more specifically, to breaking out of what we might call one's own personal mold: the personality breaks out of the person. A situation of lawlessness.

Such are the banalities that occupy my time. I can even make them precisely what they are: word games. Such trivialities I trill! Odious odysseys of words, oh Dios!

Even so, and seriously... what is the thing that eludes me, the thing that is disturbed: my personality or my person?

Labyrinths.

From the spot where a refrigerator, beds, tables, and chairs came out, another, bigger refrigerator, more chairs, and more tables are going into the house with three courtyards.

Above the double doorway they've put up the crest of a sports team and to each side of it they've hung small lanterns, both suspended from their electric cords. The lanterns seem to hold out an invitation to nocturnal adventure.

The nature of the establishment's activity is unforeseeable: Will it be cloaked in the discretion of a clandestine gambling den or will it spend every night tossing foulmouthed or crooning drunkards out onto the sidewalk? The third alternative would be some kind of tranquil social club, with normal, cheerful comings and goings. The latter possibility is ruled out by the size of the bar and some of the tables: the round ones covered in green baize.

I step off the tram and, as always, enter my street with a searching gaze that extends as far as my house. Sometimes, more from the colors of their clothing than anything else, I can distinguish Nina with our child in her arms on the bridge across the acequia.

Today is different: There's a sort of tendril that has emerged, a new development. A square sign is sticking out from the club, as if to stop the passerby in his tracks. I can't yet read what it says, but its shape is ominous.

Closer up, I can see.

GRAND OPENING DANCES
SATURDAY AND SUNDAY

Imposed music.

I seem to feel something that cannot be: as if the perfect equilibrium of the lobes of my brain had been altered by a slight collapse of the left one.

Even if that didn't happen, it's still costing me considerable effort to set my feet down, one after the other. The normal sounds of late afternoon are distorted; I have to focus my gaze so things don't lose their clarity. An attempt to speak would be like speaking for the first time, an apprenticeship.

I believe this is fear. I am afraid.

By the time I reach the house I'm no longer paralyzed with trepidation. But there's still a violence I'm barely able to contain.

Oh, may everything go well tonight, may no one contradict me.

It's Saturday and I'm spying on the dance. I need to know how far they'll go: whether the six vocalists with their three orchestras will sing only to the house with the three courtyards or will also be amplified into the surrounding neighborhood. I must watch to see how many people go in: if it's a failure they won't do it every Saturday and Sunday to come.

Many cars and the kind of vehicle called a jeep arrive, along with trucks and motorcycles. Throngs come on foot.

The orchestras don't play too loudly, only just enough for their sound to expand across the courtyard's open air.

That week's fear (the attack that overcame me) was premature. Still, it was the inevitable reaction to a sudden signal, warning that everything was about to begin again.

Up, up, up! Loud music bursts out into the air. From loudspeakers every bit as powerful as my fear foretold.

Midnight. Nina comes up to my little room with something to say. But I notice she holds back when she sees me.

I tell her to come out with it. "The baby's scared. He's crying. He doesn't want to sleep," she says.

The dances are a success. Thursdays and holidays are added to the schedule along with Saturdays and Sundays.

The little boy is used to it now, and sleeps. I don't.

At first I tried to stay away. Now I'm at war.

On nights when there was a dance, I traded my home for the cinema or the theater. Afterward I took my time going back, sitting in the haze of a café, or wandering alone through plazas that were somehow still situated in my adolescence. There were also sporadic late-night screenings, movies that helped shrink the long bouts of insomnia in my bed beneath the loudspeakers. Which stayed on until four in the morning.

No more. Now I keep watch and wage war.

The noise nuisance ordinance says: "Dances. With amplification, until two a.m. Without, until four a.m."

Nevertheless, the "with" schedule is applied all the way through the "without" schedule, and beyond, to when there is no schedule.

With respect to the situation that was keeping me awake, I visited the commanding officer of the local police station. The commander looked at me the way a person looks at an additional job that must be done. Then, with the air of a man of great tolerance performing an act of charity, he gave orders.

As a result, the loudspeakers have been restricted to the legal schedule. Even so, I have to monitor them closely. The revelers are quite brazen, and may be deliberately seeking to irritate me.

Yesterday they succeeded. It was two thirty in the morning and they were still going strong. I went to the police station. (It was easy: I was already up. I stand in my room, reading, deafened by the wax earplugs, for as long as the siege persists.)

The officer on duty told me, "We have to be tolerant... They're having fun." Then he grasped that I wasn't sharing in the fun and announced, "I'm sending over the order." I think he was only trying to get rid of me. The loudspeakers went on for another hour. On Monday I'll pay the commander another visit.

The ordinance states: "In order to minimize resonance outside the building, dance floor, or courtyard where the sound is produced, the loudspeakers must be tilted towards the ground at an angle of x degrees."

I present myself at the municipal offices to request an inspection.

These are defensive tactics. The scourge of noise is diminished by no more than a few decibels.

I could kill—in the crime novel I write prior to *The Roof*— the club's president.

But they'd only close their doors for forty-eight hours or so and cancel the first but not the second dance, which would be in celebration of their new president.

Perhaps the homicide would have some kind of intimidating efficacy if I told them in an anonymous letter that it was because of the noise they make. But that very letter would give me away; my name is known to the local police as that of a combatant against noise.

I don't understand myself when I return from these farcical flights of imagination. Why do I give myself over to them, integrate myself into their plotline? Am I using them to reduce or redirect my bitterness?

Do I bifurcate myself, or pretend to, so as to compensate? I don't know.

My head hurts. Not all of it, just one side. As if a wire were running from my forehead down through that side, a wire that is electrified or on fire.

———

I'm wary of Besarión, though he approaches me only at long intervals.

He's free. He has managed to make his life a long digression, or a kind of multiple metaphor.

I still have my yearnings, my ambitious visions. I do everything everyone else does at home and at the office, and I will write a book (two books).

In the way he dresses, you can see the absence of his mother's care—his mother whom he never mentions now, perhaps to preserve his memories and feelings from other people's clutches.

His clothing is incoherent—garments that bear no relation to one another. I say this to him whenever we see each other. He explains, "They're spoils."

"They're not worn-out."

"Spoils of the trip, from many countries."

"Many? It wasn't only Switzerland?"

"Another trip. The long journey I went on afterwards."

Besarión says he has been on a bewildered pilgrimage, in quest of the signal.

"What is—or was—it supposed to be, this signal?"

"Unforeseeable. A smile from the Virgin of Macarena, perhaps."

"And were you granted that smile?"

"I gazed at her until I could no longer see her face. But my exaltation drifted off course. Without taking my eyes off her, I was distracted. I remembered certain names I'd just heard in the streets of Andalusia, names that were new to me: the Rubio, the sun; the Sartén, the valley in the fiery sun of afternoon; the Verdugo, a famous murderous or vengeful bull, and by extension any bull that kills a bullfighter; the Gitanilla, the little gypsy, who is the Virgin of Macarena, because of her olive skin. I promised myself I'd come back. As I left my spot, I asked the girl who was praying next to me to excuse me as I slipped by her. She raised her head. Her skin was olive, and her lips and eyes smiled at me."

"In Reims there's an angel who's always smiling."

"Exactly. In his case, I hoped he might stop smiling, for an instant, for me. From the Black Madonna and Child I wanted a movement."

"Black Madonna and Black Child . . . in Africa?"

"No. In Einsiedeln, beneath a baroque ceiling that looks as if it's flying away and carrying us off with it. In Saint Mark's Basilica I felt anxious contemplating the nails and thorns of the Cross, then closed my eyes and tried to induce the wounds of the flesh in myself. (I deserve them.)

"Rome, too, was burning—beneath the sun—when I was there. I felt unwashed and uncomfortable. At Saint Peter's I cooled off in the fountain, and then in the shade of the apse and the nave. I didn't kiss the statue's bronze foot, worn down by the lips of pilgrims. I wasn't seeking pardon or indulgence, only the signal. I leaned back against the marble semicircle that sets off the steps down to Saint Peter's tomb, to watch two workers on the cathedral crossing, so high above I couldn't see where they put their feet down or even if they put them down.

"At that moment I heard a fly buzzing. It flew in front of my eyes and disappeared. I said to myself, 'It followed me in. There are no flies here, there can't be, it's too dark and everything's clean. There's no food.' When it buzzed back I had no doubt that it was there for me. Then I thought, 'If there can be no flies here, but there is one, and it chooses me among all the people here, isn't this fly, might this fly not be, the signal?' The joy of being rewarded came to me and along with it an eagerness for fuller revelation of the signal, even though the creature consecrated as its agent revolted me. Suddenly I felt it on my neck and the revulsion was stronger than I was. I gave a hard slap and killed it. I shook my shirt out and it fell to the ground. I knelt down to look at it, and brooded on it for an immense lapse of time, I don't know how long. It no longer was, or never had been, a fly. It was a bee, a golden bee."

———

It's not my finger on the trigger. Still, the air gun, instrument of my twelve-year-old cruelty to cats, fires.

From the other bedroom, my mother's voice startles us. "Those are gunshots."

"I know. Shots from an air gun, a matagatos."

No. Shots from a revolver. There across the way, at dawn.

We hear a car making its getaway. We see a man sprawled on his stomach. His hat is still on, he's dressed all in blue, and a red stain is growing on the seat of his pants, devouring their color. He moans. Another man, nearby, is sacrificing a few drops of blood to the earth in exchange for every step he takes. The price grows steeper until he's spent all he had.

The subsequent news coverage conceals as much as it reveals, and features women, cards, and dice.

The scandal doesn't fan the club's flames, it puts them out. It's that big.

A light wakes me up. Nina is cradling the child.

"What's happening?" I ask, emerging from the cave of sleep.

Nina says nothing but goes on soothing the child's tears.

Later, beside me, and I believe somewhat resentfully, she says, "Only some noises bother you."

I subject the kernel of reproach in her statement to careful scrutiny. Nina bears the great fatigue of the whole day in her body. At night, the child cries. It ruins her sleep, while I don't even hear it.

I share some conclusions reached during an earlier meditation. "Nina, sounds that are made by the little one, because he's our little one, are beloved sounds. They don't hurt me."

This isn't taking me where I'm trying to go. I say more. "It's like the bucket knocking against the mosaic tiles while the floor is mopped, the plates, the clink of crockery against crockery for an hour, twice a day. They do make sounds, sounds that could disturb my siesta or my reading. But they don't, they don't affect me, I don't hear them. They're not excessive, and they're made by someone I love."

I turn, seeking her understanding, but Nina has covered her head with the bedspread.

Even without the club across the way, the pain comes, again and again.

Children have built wooden soap-box cars with metal wheels. One child sits on the thing, another pushes it, and the little car races down the street, its hard wheels rattling and scraping against the concrete.

The wire in my head switches on and that whole side becomes sensitive.

Angry, loving mothers stick their heads out of windows to scold their offspring—"One of these days a car's going to run you kids over!"—and order them out of the street.

The children obey, leaving the street and carrying the soap-box car to the sidewalk, where its solid metal wheels strike and grind once more, now into the cracks between the cement paving stones.

The doctor exonerates noise, diagnosing neuralgia instead. He allows me some pills.

He doesn't listen and doesn't understand, I think.

I ask whether it would be prudent—and in asking, I am prudent—for me to consult a specialist. He replies that if I know so much, why did I consult him?

In consternation I contemplate the changes unleashed across the street.

The house with three courtyards is undergoing a commercial subdivision and assuming a new identity as a mixture of furniture store, tailoring shop, and repair shop for motorcycles and motor scooters.

When, without knowing it, I was furnishing the basis for Reato's candidacy for the city council with my notes and newspaper clippings, the editor in chief of his paper wanted to meet the purveyor of the campaign against noise. He was not kind. He pointed out that my contribution was flimsy and incomplete, as if to discourage me were I, on that basis alone, to aspire to consider myself a journalist.

He argued with me. "You attack auto-body shops, metal-workers, and the loudspeakers at dance halls. They're not the worst. The most calamitous noise of all is made by motorcycles."

I had them all classified in my head and responded tersely. "No, señor. Motorcycle noise is transient."

But I now judge the matter differently. Because the motorcycles park across the way, and their exhaust pipes backfire when they arrive, when they leave, and while they're being repaired. They travel back and forth across the same hundred meters like horses at exercise, their thunder pounding the air. I know this now because the motorcycle- and scooter-repair shop took over the front of the house with three courtyards, then gradually conquered the sidewalk and the street as well.

Around the corner, the street is a vast platform for the stalls of the farmers market that operates from seven in the morning until two in the afternoon. The market, too, has its loudspeaker and whoever administers it has only a few overworked records to play and a considerable number of advertisements to read out.

A carapace of music protects me, the one my mother invented in the first house that was invaded. Good classical music, rational, measured, peaceful.

It plays on the state radio station but not always when I need it. I have records, too, which are available at irregular hours.

But the stereo console is part of the dining-room-furniture set, and my family does not relish sustained exposure to its music, or so it appears. The device is bulky, not easily moved up and down the stairs. I ask my cousin for energy-saving ideas. My cousin, who knows about these things, builds an oscillator and attaches it to a cheap radio from 1930.

I stack up a pile of long-playing records, reduce the volume of the stereo to an inaudible level, and my oscillator, upstairs, captures the music as if it were a little receiver. Through the amplifier of the 1930 radio, I have music at exactly the volume I want.

Of course I have to be sure the record changer is working properly, otherwise the whole system breaks down, and also that the oscillator doesn't lose the signal, as it does a couple of times every two or three minutes.

I suppose in the end I'll opt for the fan. At least during the night. In a field alongside the Avenida de Acceso, an amusement park has been established. The noise from its rides and loudspeakers rises like smoke from a bonfire and expands on high to spiral around my room.

We thought the fan was beyond repair. It has a defective blade; as it spins, it threatens to break off, fly away, and slit someone's throat. That doesn't matter, because the noise it produces when it hits against the spokes submerges all others. The clickety-clack of the broken blade has lost all power to exasperate. Its dull monotony blankets me. Sometimes it even lulls me to sleep.

———

In the street, I cross paths with Reato.

I hide my rancor, but not my contempt. He accepts it.

He asks me things, among them what it is that I have, the thing that he sees in me but can't seem to define.

"It hurts here," I say, and repeat an action that brings me some relief: I slide the tips of my fingers along above my temples, exerting pressure.

"The noise," he diagnoses, with a hard glint of something I don't understand.

"What…?"

"The noise has gotten into your head."

So he knows. There aren't many who do. I can't reply.

I'm uneasy and ask him to tell me something I don't have the slightest interest in knowing: Which section does he write for now, which column is his? I haven't read anything lately that sounds like him.

He tells me he's moved to a different paper and is now writing brief items about sensational events. He's working on a series about spaceships.

He wants to know what I think of that, whether I approve.

"Of your work? I don't know. I haven't read it."

"No, of the flights to the moon, to Mars."

"Yes, I think so. It's the conquest of space, isn't it?"

"But we haven't conquered the earth, where we live!"

"I think we have. There's almost nothing left to explore."

"By no means. We share the earth with sickness, hunger, ignorance. Every spaceship, every flight, costs an incalculable fortune. Think of it! What if that money were spent building housing, doing research on the deadly diseases we consider incurable?"

I think, rather, of an invisible cloud that could envelop each one of us to defend us from changes in temperature, harmful gases, certain contagions, and noise. But I tell Reato his reasoning would be acceptable if the spirit of science and adventure didn't justify the journey to the moon before all the woes of earth are remedied, just as Columbus came to

America while in Europe everyone spent their lives crouched at the ready to pillage each other.

Reato reckons it's not the same thing, that those on one side and on the other build their spaceships to reach dead or unborn worlds at a cost that isn't comparable to that incurred by Columbus or Marco Polo. He lashes back at me. "You say I'm resisting mankind's advancement. But it's you who are the enemy of progress!"

"Me?"

"Yes. You want all repair shops to disappear, the garages that fix cars, buses, trucks, and ambulances so they can supply you with food and transport you, whether you're alive, sick, or dead."

I try to say I don't want to eliminate them, I only want them out of areas where people live, but Reato doesn't let me. He strikes out at me (with words): "Yes, dead! Tell the truth, you've thought about killing yourself, haven't you? That way you won't hear any more noise."

And he lets out a braying bellow of laughter.

I hit him with my hand. I hit his mouth. I had a bunch of keys in my hand.

He's bleeding and he hates me. I appall him. He flees.

I perceive the city reconstituting itself around me. Some faces condemn me, others evince wariness of my strength or my fury. But no one is impeding my movements. I know that can't last: I leave.

In fact, that's the only escape I hadn't thought of: my own death.

I believed—the things one reads—that eternity was the endless sequence of instants.

In the contemplative hours of adolescence, the instants made themselves visible to me as thin circular wafers or very flat lozenges with surfaces of polished gold. Time soaked through them, one by one, but their continuous procession never ended; this was communication with the infinite, and each little disk, as it emerged, was magnificent in and of itself.

I've been living from moment to moment ever since, but I've never again seen one of those gilded lozenges, and from the next instant the world delivers to me I expect nothing but its burden of adversity. (Neither love nor hope is absent, but they won't be given to me, and that's on me.)

Now I believe I've also lost track of the meaning of eternity.

Or I keep myself from trying to find its meaning, limit myself to thinking, with extreme simplicity, that eternity is life going on until it's gone on too long, suffering all the while, yet lacking the will to go beyond.

Last night, I had my twelve-year-old self's matagatos gun in my hands again.

From my tower, I pointed it at someone, I have no way of knowing who, someone who must have been about to pass by, down there on the street. The street went along, inert and hollow, and I was full of despair, foreseeing that I had to kill someone then and there, whoever it might be, even if I had to turn the weapon against myself.

I looked at the street, calm and empty to infinity, and assured myself I heard no footsteps, no horses bearing a single rider or drawing a carriage, and then, since I couldn't go on like that any longer, I shot the matagatos into my ear, aiming for my brain. I heard it fire, my hand dropped from the cloud of spent gunpowder, and my body remained standing and alive. From the windowsill rose a spiky black bird I hadn't noticed until then. It opened its beak and no doubt let out a caw but I didn't hear a sound.

The bullet destroyed my ear (a single bullet destroyed both ears and my hearing), without continuing on into the brain, without killing me. I was deaf.

I can't remember whether I was happy too.

———

The recent widow needed to shore up her finances, I know, so she decided to rent out the garage. Yes, but...

The rented garage is the next entrance on the street, after the front gate of my house. Since this morning, bit by bit, a small shop that will fix radios, record players, speakers, and TV sets has been settling in there.

There are two young men wearing heavy knit sweaters in complex, showy patterns. I've seen them. They're building shelves. They whistle and open boxes that are full of things.

They haven't gone to lunch, it appears, or they're having cold cuts from the grocery store. They're in a hurry, anticipating the regular operation of their business: an American stereo, playing music also from America, stands on the sidewalk.

The installation ends early (or is left to only one of the men). The other turns his attention to the first receiver in need of surgery. The device, I almost want to believe, struggles and resists, emitting squeals of pain that are extremely high-pitched, extremely piercing.

I laugh to myself, or smile, shaking my head, telling myself that I understand, that I have to be stoic, that one day, like the club before it, the little repair shop, too, will be gone.

I neglect to think about all the rest of it. Still, other questions rush forward to present themselves to my consciousness: And the rattling and backfiring of cars and buses? And the vociferating loudspeaker at the farmers market around the corner? And the grinding of the amusement park's gears...?

The wire, just above my temple, starts emitting its signals. I pay no attention to it for a while, and it rages, vibrates, turns white-hot, until the pain makes me cry out and weep. I'm weeping.

My wife knows about the sedative. She gives me so much that all at once, just like that, I go to sleep. The abyss calls to me...

I'm in bed, in my bed. It's daytime, four in the afternoon, and I hear voices from the ether, snatches of voices. (I know already: the little repair shop right next door.)

I've slept nineteen hours.

The doctor woke me up. He said: It's nothing.

When I explained to him, judiciously, that I find myself predisposed towards whatever will come, whatever must come, his manner changed. He told me he may have to remove the inflamed nerve, or give me an injection "a little painful, also in that nerve. You'll remember it afterwards as an injection of milk."

Tomorrow I'll be able to go back to work.

I go downstairs to light the gas water heater; I'm going to take a bath.

The kitchen's drawn blinds establish a penumbra that isn't too dense. I don't need to switch on the light.

A late fly is buzzing around angrily because it can't find an exit.

I lower the burning match and the little fountain of blue forms on the gas burner.

The fly brushes past me in direct, demented flight: it saw light and does not know that it is fire. It enters, and for an instant tiny orange flames dance around inside the blue fountain.

I raise the blinds so daylight can illuminate me. On the granite floor lies the fly, still and wingless.

I recover the ancestral notion of cleansing, destructive fire.

I save it as a memory, the type of memory that suddenly clears everything up.

Because I cannot kill. I mean, I cannot scrutinize those young men as potential victims if I'm the one who has to be the murderer. (I'm thinking about the book, understand.)

———

Some animals scrabble around in earth or sand to take refuge or procreate, to store food or seek it. Some men scrabble around among wheels and motors stilled and rusted by rain. I was one of those men, and there I found the soul of the instrument I needed to launch sound into battle against sound.

I took my cousin the impossible find: the ignition coil of a Ford Model T.

Now I have to wait. He's building it.

My sloppy, lying-around-the-house attire and nonchalant cigarettes camouflage my espionage mission as a casual stroll.

I note the points where the fire could spread and intensify until it does the greatest damage.

Also, how its flames could find their way inside while the person who sets it does not.

The gasoline trickles in under the door. The thread is as thin as possible on this side; once inside, it will spread out. The match is applied. There's time to reach the corner at a normal pace, make the turn, and know nothing at all about any of it.

The door is solid: no glass panes or openings. It will conceal the disaster. The telltale sign of smoke will come later: it will have to thin out before it can emerge through the cracks.

Once the gasoline has been consumed, there'll be nothing left to indicate the cause of the blaze.

The Model T ignition coil is a kind of puff pastry: sheets of iron, laid sideways. Into all that, a cardboard tube is wrapped, or unwrapped; from it emerge six or seven twisting horns, sutured in place with duct tape.

Dangling from the coil is a variable capacitator that my cousin has attached, but the capacitator's destiny was already linked to the coil by a cable, and it hangs, dancing in the air, never completing its fall.

To the coil, my cousin joins two slender, modern filaments, covered in shiny, brightly colored plastic. He raises them and folds them so their tips converge but don't touch.

From the coil he picks up the cord that ends in a plug and plugs it in. With a high-pitched hiss, a small, unstable spark forms between the converging tips of the filaments. He unplugs it.

"There you go," my cousin says.

Maybe.

With another cable, he connects the coil to a radio receiver. He starts turning the dial, ordering me to pay close attention. In the house next door—we're at my cousin's house—a radio delivers itself up to its garrulous purpose.

My cousin spins the dial. He says, "You have to find the same station."

He finds it, the music coincides. In unison, the two houses feign being one and the same.

My cousin connects the coil. The spark jumps between the filaments. A storm breaks out inside the neighbor's radio. Violent static squawks break through the music, as if the receiver were being smashed with rocks.

Someone comes running, shouting, "What's happening to that thing?"

There's the sound of someone pounding on the console's case, a series of conjectures on the part of a pair of intrigued women, a gust of music, different music (my cousin gestures that they've changed stations), and normal reception is restored.

My cousin is at the ready, his hand on the dial. He tunes in to the various stations. He smiles and his smile says: You'll see.

He twirls the knob to the same station as the other radio. He plugs in. Chaos once more ensues.

He says again: "There you go."

This time I believe him.

Meanwhile, the commotion has suggested some catastrophe to the women on the other side of the wall. One, in great distress, wonders, "And the TV? Is it ruined too?"

They try it out.

My cousin connects his own television, sets it to the same

channel, and causes such a racket that a woman screams, "Turn it off, turn it off! The screen's exploding!"

In my house.

Nina, drying her hands, witnesses our entrance with the bundles. She says hola to my cousin and my cousin says hola. I take over the dining room table and we proceed with the unwrapping.

Nina and my mother peer in at us. I promise, euphoric: You'll see.

With a professional hand, my cousin smooths out cables, regulates the proximity of the filaments, attaches the coil to my stereo system's radio.

We wait for his ritual, which begins with a cocked ear and the recognition of the song coming from the radio in the garage next door. He captures the same song on our receiver. He plugs in. The spark bursts forth. I can see it in Nina's eyes, and in my mother's. It must have been in mine, too, even brighter.

But the song next door doesn't change.

Neither does my cousin.

He looks at the ceiling. He asks if I still have the architectural plans for the house. I say: Yes, what for?

I bring them in and he looks them over and renders a conclusive diagnosis. "As I suspected. Lots of metal. You've got a whole gridiron of rebar up there overhead. It will never let the waves through."

I propose one last hope. "What if we do it from the little room upstairs? It's up above the gridiron."

My cousin is not a man of hurried responses. He consults the plans. He says, "The little room sits eight meters above the sidewalk, plus two or three meters more of oblique deviation towards the garage makes ten, possibly eleven. Too much space for the jammer to reach across."

Too much. For me.

They've assembled a loudspeaker from a kit or built it out of spare parts. I don't know.

They're testing its output levels. The sound reaches my house. I imagine it reaches many houses.

With parsimonious English arithmetic, they investigate certain of its effects: *One, two, three, four, five...*

They desist from their verbalizations and hand the work over to a record. Many records. The loudspeaker amplifies them.

Driven by the same instinct that makes us probe our own wounds, I stick my head outside to have a look.

They've put it up high on top of a crate on the sidewalk.

My wire, violated, vibrates. Demands I do something.

A policeman is coming, weighted with weaponry. I'll say, "You've got to do something, Officer."

But that can't be. I must grit my teeth and bear up. If I use a policeman to silence the loudspeaker, I'll be marked as the man who launched an attack on the radio-repair shop. I mustn't create antecedents that will be used against me.

I go inside, close the windows, and shut myself away with my wire.

The loudspeaker falls silent. Only the occasional growl of a passing scooter comes through the windowpanes' weak protection.

If the loudspeaker comes back, I'll get dressed and go down and file a complaint with the police. It doesn't matter if, in my head, I ruin the defense of the character I'm re-searching for my novel. I know it's my experience that is bringing him to life, and if I limit it he'll vanish, but I'm the author of the book, not the man who'll set the fire. I need for my wire to calm down.

He's wearing worn-out gray overalls and his beard clearly wasn't grown on purpose. But it's him; it's Besarión, coming toward me with his mind alert and shining from his eyes, in contradiction of the shabby figure he cuts, though his eyes aren't focused on anything specific.

I sidestep him. Not because I'm afraid he'll make me practice a little out-of-pocket charity. Because of the cane.

He'll ask me some question and I won't be able to deceive him the way I deceived Nina and my mother. I told them, "It's a precaution the doctor ordered so I can keep my balance if, on top of the pain, I have vertigo."

But I'd have to tell Besarión the truth: that I'm taking advantage of my condition to try to avoid his mistake. His nerves were rattled and he gave the slap that killed the bug without knowing whether it was a fly or a bee. If my nerves are rattled and I start telling people off over the loudspeak-ers or the motorcycles, I might be attacked. If they attack me, I might deliver a terrible blow: seize whatever's at hand and perhaps even kill. With the cane in my hand I know I can tell them off in the certainty that—dear God—I will not kill. I'll deliver a good thrashing, no more.

With deep shame, I'm apologizing: Besarión saw me dodge him, pretend not to recognize him.

I've humiliated him.

There's a certain squalor inside me . . .

*

I head home. I know a source of noise lurks there (of the noise man makes with his machines).

I'm still at a distance, which keeps me from hearing the noises . . . Yet already the distress and beleaguerment are building up inside me! It must be that other noise, the ambushing noise that can't be heard, the one that emanates from people.

Long before this, when I lived with my mother, Besarión gave me his diagnosis. "Your quest against noise is metaphysical."

"Why do you say that . . . ? I don't understand. I know nothing at all about that subject."

He pretended to be in the know. "You hear metaphysical noises."

"But Besarión, what are metaphysical noises?"

Besarión said, "Those that act upon your being."

(My mind would return to these ideas of his again and again; that was how he began working his way into my thinking.)

I took a few moments to absorb this statement, which he delivered as a profound conclusion. I allowed myself to be convinced. I fell to musing. "Noises that act upon my being . . . or that don't permit me to find it, so I can't identify myself with my being."

I don't know whether my next thought, which I found judicious, debased the quality of my meditation or confused the metaphysical noise Besarión spoke of with other noises, but I added, still only to myself: "Noise distracts me, takes me out of myself . . . but is that me being separated from my being, or simply being driven mad?"

Nevertheless, on that same occasion, Besarión either developed his ideas further or set a trap, because he soon discounted the importance of his previous assessment and changed his argument. "Your adventure is metaphysical, even if its results are alien to anything philosophical, because you knit it from subtle elements, or out of nothing, mostly in your head."

This now seemed like contempt or incomprehension. Still, I allowed him to continue: "But you're mistaken or exaggerating. Your disorder is physiological, or psychic, or nervous. Physiology, not metaphysics."

I defended myself. "I've never aspired to give my problem any titles of nobility. You were the one who brought up metaphysics, not me."

"Don't be offended," he said, conciliatory. "And don't suppose I think you're a sick man, either."

I understood. I justified him. "I give people reason to believe that . . . And it could happen, my health could fail, I could become unbalanced. I acknowledge that, all of it. Luckily, I've been enduring this martyrdom without falling sick. I'm a healthy man, in mind and body.

"And yes, it would humiliate me to be conscious of being merely a sick man, nothing more than that. That is, if I no longer aspired to anything greater, which isn't the case.

"The bad thing"—I was beginning to truly torment myself, without being ashamed of doing so in front of my friend— "is that the noise won't let me do what I want. The noise won't let me . . ."—I was going to say "won't let me be," but I said "won't let me exist."

Yet that seemed far too intellectual and pretentious a phrase. I corrected myself a little, "won't let me exist, barely lets me live," and it came out even worse.

These confessions may have annoyed Besarión, whose reply was quick and sharp. "It lets you live. Bear up. Make do."

"I act upon other people," I concluded, and resolved to steer clear of any feelings of anger towards Besarión and of continued discussion of the subject.

I believe I felt as if this confession had betrayed my sense of modesty. I decided to forget the entire exchange.

I haven't managed to, particularly not the sarcastic line: "Your quest is metaphysical . . . You knit it from subtle elements, or out of nothing, mostly in your head."

"Lighter fluid."

The curved, stubby flask resembles those used for whisky or cognac, in a shape adapted to the back pockets of pants.

At the pharmacy: "A rubber syringe bulb."

"Large?"

"No, small. One that can fit in my jacket pocket."

I pass by the kitchen. My mother is knitting. Nina is feeding the child.

I go up to the bathroom.

I fill the bulb with water. I leave the room, shutting the door. I introduce the tip of the bulb under the door and squeeze the water out. I open the door and observe. The water hasn't followed a direct course, as the position of the tip made me imagine it would; it has run off in another direction, following the slope of the floor.

That will need to be taken into account. For example, if the most valuable part of the bathroom were that little stool over there, I'd have to inject the gasoline (or lighter fluid) by aiming the syringe bulb over towards this side, and not down the middle.

The fluid, like gasoline, combusts rapidly, or so I believe. I must put that to the test. I'm not certain, because in the cigarette lighter I don't see it burning; it's the wick that burns.

To keep from doing any damage and ensure that it burns nothing when it burns, I pour a little of the fluid over the sink's concave porcelain.

I toss in a match.

Instantly a flash and a boom explode up at me.

The pain is suddenly there, twisting above my temple. Shouts come running.

I stand in front of the mirror recovering my own reflection, which had become watery or vaporous a moment earlier.

The mirror shows me the fear and anxiety in their faces as Nina and my mother come bursting in to save me.

"What was that? What happened?" Their emotion is still frenzied, wanting to know.

I say, "Nothing. I washed my hands in alcohol but didn't rinse with water. Then I forgot about it, lit a cigarette, and tossed the match into the sink."

"And the bomb?"

"Bomb?" I laugh. "The fumes and flame in the sink's drainpipe erupted all at once and with a boom."

Nina is visibly bewildered. "How can that be ... ?"

I go to her and run my fingers over her forehead, the way I do when I'm trying to alleviate my own pain.

She looks at me and says, sobbing, "You've scorched your eyelashes and eyebrows."

The bell at our front gate has begun ringing insistently. It must be some of the neighbors, in solidarity (and curiosity).

An afternoon paper brings word of the day's early-morning discovery: a man, aged thirty to thirty-five, with a brown beard, wearing a gray lab coat for a jacket.

The item does not say whether he did it or it was done to him, or how. It reads like a provisional notice, until someone comes forward to help identify him. That sort of assistance is precisely what it solicits.

I'll go downstairs and have dinner later on. That's usually what I do. My dinner is left waiting for me in the kitchen.

On my way, I try to visualize his gaze that morning, the only time I ever tried to dodge him. I don't find any message or warning there, and for now that spares me remorse.

I imagined men in white, doctors, perhaps a judge, his authority, his retinue. No: in this place where dead bodies are stored, the person standing guard behind the counter looks like an office worker. A uniformed officer stands nearby, making it known that he's listening in, and looking me over thoroughly without choosing to intervene. Or not yet, I think.

I thought they were all men, but in the hallway the employee hands me over to a female nurse. I'm to follow her.

I'd imagined a subterranean place and a kind of big, crowded refrigerator. It may well be like that. I never find out because I don't get very far inside. The nurse assigns me to a white chair made of metal.

The policeman arrives. He knows what time it is and he isn't in any hurry. He accompanies me into a little room.

There he is. He looks exactly like himself, grown tender and innocent.

I work up the nerve to voice the question of whether he himself was the one who wanted this.

The nurse's reply is both vulgar and sweet. "He froze to death. Poor man, he reminds me of a little bird."

"Yes," I say.

The policeman asks, "Is it him ... ?"

I say, "I believe so."

"You believe ... ? You aren't sure?"

"I said: I believe."

This time I follow the policeman. Back at the counter he uses the telephone. The judge on the other end of the line has him ask me whether Besarión had any family here in the city. And could they be summoned immediately, for an identification at ten-thirty p.m., in his presence. I say: I believe so.

The policeman hangs up. The policeman tells me I can't leave. I protest: Home to dinner, then I'll be back.

While he's looking up the two sisters' numbers in the phone book, he concedes. "If you feel like having something to eat, you're free to go. There's a place across the way, through the garden."

It's a little bar. I order a sandwich and glance around at the men drinking wine. The owner looks at me, as if resigned to hearing a story, the kind of story people tell when they're in a fix. Where I've come from and what, more or less, is keeping me waiting here are visible to all, or so it seems. Even so, I don't speak. I go on looking around. I distract myself.

Alerted by the clock, I cross the street and go through the garden. Two cars outside weren't there when I left. I'll meet the two sisters in the front office. I wonder whether to offer my condolences then or to wait until after they've seen him.

There are four people: the two women and their two husbands. It's obvious these are the husbands, though I've never met them.

I say buenas noches. Only one of the men says buenas and the rest of them give a slight nod. Which means I should stand to one side and wait.

They don't speak, they don't weep, they show no concern over the judge's failure to arrive on time. They don't look at me. If they don't look at me, it's because they can guess that I was the one who supplied their names and their relationship to the deceased.

At eleven p.m. the shift changes. The departing policeman says hasta mañana to me. I don't know what he thinks will happen tomorrow.

The judge arrives with a scant retinue, just one secretary. We rise to our feet and he greets us briefly as he gusts through like a strong wind.

Later he calls for us.

The sisters bend forward to look, but not too much. They glance at each other in consultation. One initiates a movement of the head to indicate no. The judge understands but wants them to say it. They say, "No, Your Honor. It's not him."

Then the judge has me step forward. He asks and I say, "I believe that it is."

They don't dispute what I say. They exchange glances among sisters and husbands, establishing an agreement to have nothing to do with this, as if Besarión—whether or not it's him lying there—were a creature of my imagination and they were leaving him in my hands.

There are other formalities. As the secretary asks each of us, in turn, for our address, to write it down, I realize that mine won't be of much use to them. Still, they have many means for locating me at their disposal. One of those means involves my fingertips, I suppose. But I don't ask.

I feel full of nothing...

I tell myself that the city ends somewhere, in a place where everyone sleeps at night.

A tram bears me towards that indeterminate periphery. Then I walk. I've lost the cane somewhere.

I come upon plaza after plaza where couples are managing to survive the cold, street corners inflamed with alcoholic fervor, little coffee shops where truco is played for beans amid impassioned sports talk.

Ghostly minibuses sleep in a caravan along the gutter, where the light fades.

One dog growls, another barks at me. A few more approach warily. I still have the afternoon paper in my pocket. I unfold it, light it, fan it, and the flames roar up. I let go and it falls, drifting, in an enormous blaze. The dogs howl as if they were being punished and abandon their pursuit.

If I were to meet Besarión somewhere in these outskirts and he were to ask where I've been, I'd stand in profile, stretch out an arm, point into the depths of this neighborhood, and say, "Over there."

And if I, in turn, were to question him, to try to learn where he is right now, would his answer be "Further beyond…"?

I think of the beyond and imagine an incorruptible silence.

Who could carry noise there…? The makers of noise are the ones present here.

Souls that drag in their wake not their own howling torment, like the ghosts in old tales, but bolts and screws.

Or they drag along their metaphysical noise, as Besarión would say mockingly.

Poor Besarión.

146 · ANTONIO DI BENEDETTO

*

Hunger comes. But I foresee that the time between my ar-
rival home and the moment when I sit down to eat will be
measured by the tail end of whatever event has placed ve-
hicles and people around my house, or nearby.

A streetlamp's jet of petrified light disturbs me.

On the corner, a huge snake has dragged itself down the
street. It is—or has been—drinking. The fireman who looks
after it on this end calms my apprehensions: It's not my
house. It's the one next door, the widow's house: the little
repair shop and also the bedrooms.

It all happened already; they're no longer spraying water.
The wounded (or burned) have been taken away, two of
them.

Someone, a stranger to me, recognizes me and sounds a
warning. "Here he comes."

From the group my wife emerges. She's sobbing. Which
doesn't mean anything in particular. It's a frequent occur-
rence lately, and tonight she has good reason for doing so.

I ask her about the child and my mother. Her answer is
strange: So now I'm thinking about them. On top of which
she reproaches me, "You should have done that before ... !"

I note that I'm surrounded, but only by pushy onlookers.
The police officer's air of expectation cloaks a different meaning, one I perceive clearly.

———

I'm alone, with the back of a uniformed officer in the doorway, in an unoccupied office, flooded with white light.

Every time they ask, I've said no, it wasn't me. They don't

insist. Still, they notice the singed lashes and brows, and their gaze lingers.

I don't defend myself.

A memory has taken hold of me, the memory of something I read, and I repeat it in my head as best I can. *In this respect, truly, if in no other, I believe I have something in common with Socrates. For when he was accused and was about to be judged ... his daemon forbade him to defend himself.*

Some words may be missing, or perhaps I'm changing some, but when I begin again, it's always these words and no other.

I don't know what my daemon might be, or what a daemon is or how it looks. But there's something that prevents me from bolstering my simple negation with arguments.

Nina has abandoned me. I understand. Living as we do, the feelings have gradually worn away.

Tomorrow the special vehicle will come. It will drive into the rear courtyard of police headquarters. I'll be its passenger, perhaps the only one for the whole journey, I don't know. When they tell me to get out, I'll be at the prison.

My mother knows what's happening.

She reprimands me. "If only you'd defend yourself!"

I'm aware that I speak as Besarión would. "Martyrs can't defend themselves. No one listens."

She doesn't say so, but my boast astonishes her and it shows.

"Martyr for having aspired to live my own life, and not someone else's, not the life that is imposed," my justification clamors within me.

But I don't speak it aloud.

*

He'll make the journey with me. Meanwhile, we share the bench under the colonnade, in the guard's shadow. Though he shrinks away, rejecting me.

I remain under the observation of the students and employees who are earning their certificates of good conduct.

I had a certificate from that class. It expired. If I wanted another one, I'd have to have my conduct certified again. Some of us always have to provide proof. I'm not doing that now. But now I'm excluded.

An absorbed gaze gravitates towards me. It comes from that girl. I look at her. She sees me looking at her and averts her eyes. Maybe it's not compassion. Maybe she's ashamed of my condition.

Yes, it's absurd. To sequester yourself from freedom is absurd.

She's gone now. But I have to think about her gaze. It didn't agitate the bad part of my being.

The special vehicle backs in, and prison guards get out.

They recognize the man next to me. "Again?"

He's defiant. "It won't be for long."

I recall his story, heard in the sunlight of the recreation yard during these days of unkempt coexistence. He's a cat burglar who glides nimbly across rooftops. They call him "the roofer." A jailer who didn't know the reason for the nickname put him on a crew that was repairing the jail's roof tiles. He slipped across that rooftop, too.

The roof...

The Roof, and all my higher ambitions, come back to me, just as dignity came back a moment ago.

"It won't be for long."

And may that time, favored by the silence of internment, be spent on something entirely noble: writing the pages that will, at last, be the beginning of my book.

They tell us to get out. I step across the gravel and know myself to be naked beneath the sun.

We're corralled through the admission procedure. Our bodies are delivered by someone, and someone else receives them. We ourselves simply bear witness to the transaction.

I hear music.

They take away our clothes and give us each a pair of pants and a zippered jacket, a mattress, a pillow, and a blanket.

I hear music. I hear voices speaking with professional locution.

It's this way: a corridor, a door made of iron bars, another corridor, another barred door.

I hear a song reaching its end. I hear the voices of male and female announcers who describe various commercial virtues in great detail.

We come out into a yard, perhaps octagonal. All of these men are standing there, idle, leaning against the wall, relaxed, talking together but acting as if they were silent. Mounted on the walls, two, no, four loudspeakers amplify the sound of a radio.

My shoulders sagging under the mattress, pillow, and blanket, I struggle from one end of the yard to the other. There's still farther to go and I'm breaking under the strain.

Here is the cell block. Inside, above the barred door, another loudspeaker imparts its information to the air I will have to breathe.

They tell me which of the beds will be mine. I set down my burden and let my arms fall and rest. I'm exposed before the prison guard. I don't know what they'll do with me now.

The guard doesn't seem to know what I'm waiting for. He tells me that if I want I can go out to the yard. They'll give me something to eat.

I'm not thinking about food. A slow movement rises through me; my fingers separate and curve over my forehead, as if each hand were gripping an apple. I ask, devastated, "And that radio . . . ?"

A good-hearted man, he answers as if it gave him joy to be able to bring me this consolation. "You like it? You'll always have it."

He can't know.

I'm sitting on a rock, on a hillside. My circumstances are pleasant, though somewhat sad.

From afar, a shepherd comes. He says, "You're not allowed to stay there."

I'm about to ask why, but he gets ahead of me. "Because a lamb was sacrificed upon this rock."

Abandoning my attitude of repose, I rise to my feet before the old man.

He's satisfied that I've obeyed and sets back on his way

Sitting on a smaller rock, I study the larger one as if it suggested an enigma to me, not a prohibition.

The sudden return of the shepherd comes as a surprise.

He reproaches me. "Don't pretend you've been given in sacrifice, or immolated!"

I'm about to reject his presumption (glimpsing, nevertheless, the truth that it reveals). I try to reproach him for his haughtiness, his indifference to my humility... But I stammer and can't manage to get it out. I'm disturbed by a sound, a new sound. It moves past. I see it as a mobile point, a golden flash in the air. A bee.

The buzzing assails me. It sits on my check, vibrating sonorously. I hit it and it falls. It's not a bee, it's a fly.

The clarity that made the dream I was dreaming so sharply etched and credible disappears. Yet the sound goes on.

I reassemble my rational mind and adapt it to the place where I am, in reality. I know already... It's the saw, operated by convicts who stay in the workshop, with special permission and for pay, until three in the morning.

I feel as if my brain had been mauled, as if it had reached the final moment of a long and selfless effort of creation. As if I'd written a book.

It is not a happy fatigue.

The night flows on ... and not toward peace.

TRANSLATOR'S AFTERWORD

IN THE year 1790, Don Diego de Zama, a high-ranking official of the Spanish Empire, marooned in Asunción, Paraguay—he hopes temporarily—tries to expand his awareness to take in the full enormity of the territory around him. "Here was I," he muses, "in the midst of a vast continent that was invisible to me though I felt it all around, a desolate paradise, far too immense for my legs. America existed for no one if not for me, but it existed only in my needs, my desires, and my fears." In Antonio Di Benedetto's 1956 novel *Zama*, America is the immense New World ruled from afar for centuries by the Spanish Crown, and Don Diego, a man born in the Empire's overseas territories, is an *americano*, an American. Though his career in the Empire's bureaucracy has been impressive, his status as an American makes him, irrevocably, the social inferior of the Spaniards around him.

Already, before it begins, the next novel Di Benedetto published, eight years later, abolishes, with a single modifier, Don Diego's anguished sense of that strange and desolate paradise that belongs to him alone. Set apart from and preceding it, like an epigraph, a brief sentence situates *The Silentiary* in the postwar years following 1950, and in a city in "América Latina." Which is no longer America itself.

In a celebrated lecture delivered in Buenos Aires in 1936, when Di Benedetto was barely a teenager, the Mexican philosopher Alfonso Reyes confronted this nomenclatural conundrum. Its title is "Notas sobre la inteligencia americana" ("Notes on the American Mind"), but in the opening line Reyes clarifies: "My observations are limited to what is called Latin America." Having established this, the lecture goes on to eschew the adjective, referring simply to America and Americans, whose unique misfortune it is, says Reyes, "to have been born and have their roots in a soil that was not the current focal point of civilization, but instead a kind of subsidiary branch of the world."

The nameless narrator of *The Silentiary* finds himself mutilated by this same specification, "limited to what is called Latin America." Like Don Diego, he chafes at local circumstances; neither the city he lives in, where he was born and grew up, nor its vast adjacent territories excite him. Traveling on his honeymoon, all he finds is more of the same. Only the fantastical European journeys of his friend Besarión, perhaps a foreigner himself, can offer the consolation of an elsewhere to complement his readings in European literature.

At the same time, another elsewhere has arrived on his doorstep and is imposing itself, invading his home. When a repair shop next door sets up a stereo system on the sidewalk, the equipment is characterized as American, and the music it broadcasts is also American. Its Americanness is alien, harsh, and grating, as is the "parsimonious English arithmetic" of the foreign words the loudspeaker repairmen repeat at high volume during their sound checks, which are, in the original Spanish, "*One, two, three, four, five...*"

Parallel intimations of an aural invasion by an alien America likewise crop up here and there in the mid-twentieth-century literature of the United States. John Updike's 1958 novel *The Poorhouse Fair* is set in a United States where

"Every other movie star was a Cuban or mestizo or something, as if you had to be brown to look like anything." The most remarkable evocation of such an invasion is "The Supremacy of Uruguay," a 1933 humor piece by E. B. White, in which a Uruguayan, inspired by a visit to Times Square, returns home to create an invincible sonic weapon: the chorus of a romantic ditty, hugely amplified and repeated ad infinitum, which quickly induces benign insanity in all who are subjected to it. The Uruguayan government mounts vast loudspeakers on swift, gleaming airplanes, and "there fell upon all the world, except Uruguay, a sound the equal of which had never been heard on land or sea." Life goes on much as usual among the subjugated peoples of the earth, except that no one can say or think anything but "thanks...for the unforgettable nights I never can replace": the weaponized song lyric. Somewhat to the Uruguayans' disappointment, none of the world's nations puts up any resistance, or even notices, in their lunacy, that Uruguay has conquered them, and "Billions dwelt contentedly in a fool's paradise." It all comes to an end when a few American children grew up, recovered their senses, "and destroyed mankind without a trace."

I first ran across White's curious little tale in Havana, while leafing through copies of the illustrated Cuban weekly *Revista Bohemia* in the archives of the national library. The issue of June 11, 1965—a year after *The Silentiary* was published—includes "La Supremacia de Uruguay" alongside vehement denunciations of the Yankee invasion of the Dominican Republic the previous month, in which thousands of Dominicans lost their lives. Some years later the U.S. troops that invaded Panama in 1989, leaving about 650 Panamanians dead in their wake, seemed to be enacting a mash-up of White's story and *The Silentiary*'s idea of "war noise" when they tried to flush Manuel Noriega out of his presidential palace by parking Humvees with loudspeakers mounted on top all around, blasting it nonstop day and night with pounding rock and roll at top volume.

The postwar era (the years 1950 and thereafter) was a period of heightened interest in silence, and in noise. In 1952, John Cage's *4'33"* was first performed in Woodstock, New York. Cage would later call this composition in three movements— of 33 seconds, 2 minutes 40 seconds, and 1 minute 20 seconds—his most important work. According to its score, "any instrumentalist or combination of instrumentalists" can perform it. The performance consists in not playing the instrument(s). The piece draws on silence and on the omnipresence of noise. (The John Cage Trust has recently made it available as an iPhone app, which features a recording of the "ambient sounds at play in John Cage's last New York apartment.") The unplayed piano the narrator of *The Silentiary* lugs from boardinghouse to boardinghouse might be an allusion to Cage's piece, or the product of a parallel line of reflection. Except that *4'33"* can be understood as a celebration of omnipresent noise, precisely the condition of existence that makes Di Benedetto's narrator's life unbearable.

At moments, the narrator wants to blame noise on the time period he lives in, the particular circumstances of postwar urban life, with its omnipresent and hypnotic stereos, loudspeakers, transistor radios, and TV sets, its defective zoning laws that allow auto-body shops in residential neighborhoods. (The urban-planning solution the narrator proposes is similar to one formulated by the architect Louis Kahn for

Philadelphia in the 1950s.) But he also resists this presentist analysis, citing an essay by Schopenhauer on disruptive noise in general and whipcracking in particular. When he and his new wife retreat to the countryside, he's inconsolable to be met with the deafening clang of the village blacksmith. There is no idyllic "before" that might be restored to solve his problem.

In a conversation that seems to flow from the pages of an Argentine novel published only two years earlier, Cage and his friend and fellow composer Morton Feldman, during a series of programs called *Radio Happenings* broadcast on WBAI in 1966 and 1967, pondered the condition of "continually being intruded upon." They agreed, to begin with, that it was not simply an issue of noisy new "hypnotic devices."

> Feldman: Years ago the radio was blaring, I think that there were just as many intrusions as there are today. But I didn't hear them. Today I hear them. So there must be something there that seems to be competing with me ... Or, let's put it this way: that my own role has been weakened psychologically.
>
> Cage: What was your role?
>
> Feldman: The old-fashioned role of the artist, deep in thought.

Against Feldman's anger and irritation, Cage contends that "This is a coin that has two sides." He cites the French composer Erik Satie, who said, "what we need is a music which will not interrupt the noises of the environment." "Say you think of your thoughts as the reality ... what you wish to have as a reality, and the environment as an intrusion," Cage asserts. "Then that Satie remark just turns it over and says the reality is the environment: what you want to do in it is an intrusion."

This coin with two sides—the reality in oneself versus the reality outside—evokes the terms of the combat established in the fourth century between Saint Anthony of Egypt and the devil, who by a series of visions tempted the saint to emerge from the sanctity of his own being, a struggle that inspired Brueghel, Flaubert, and many others. In *The Silentiary*, the unusual name of the narrator's friend, Besarión, is shared by a disciple of Saint Anthony's, Saint Bessarion of Egypt, who led the life of a wanderer and was known for having said, "I cannot live under a roof."

Early Christian ascetics were a continuing source of inspiration for Di Benedetto. In one of the best-known of his short stories, a nineteenth-century gaucho named Aballay learns about the fourth-century stylites, who lived on high pillars for the mortification of their bodies. In an act of penitence, Aballay resolves to emulate them and spend the rest of his life without ever descending from his horse. The possibility of sacrifice, mortification, and subsequent redemption comes up several times in *The Silentiary*, particularly with regard to Besarión, to whom the narrator attributes a "capacity to destroy himself for the greater good." By the end of the novel, the narrator's own capacity for sacrifice is at issue. Now incarcerated, the silentiary has a dream that alludes to the biblical story of Abraham's binding of Isaac. The dream brings in a glimmer of redemption, the notion that the narrator's action—specifically his refusal to defend himself, though innocent of the crime he's charged with—might be understood as a heroically redemptive attempt to save his mother, wife, and son from the "instrument of not-allowing-to-be" that he has become. That is, his imprisonment could be a form of expiation, a way of saving himself and his family from the crimes he has committed—against them. This possibility was one that Di Benedetto later rejected.

There's no indication that Di Benedetto thought of *Zama*, *The Silentiary*, and *The Suicides*—the novels he published in 1956, 1964, and 1969—as a trilogy. No one else, during his lifetime, seems to have suggested that the three be read that way. These were not his only novels; there were two others: his first, *El pentágono* in 1955, and his last, *Sombras, nada mas*, published in 1985, the year before his death. But many readers viewed the three middle novels as his best. And certain parallels between them, perhaps even a continuity among them, were observed. All, to begin with, are "soliloquies," as Juan José Saer points out in the introduction to *The Silentiary* he wrote thirteen years after Di Benedetto's death, where, by the authority vested in him as one of Argentina's greatest living writers, he pronounced the three novels a trilogy. The relationship thus established has endured the test of time. In 2011, the Barcelona house El Aleph Editores brought the three out in a single volume titled *Trilogia de la espera*; Adriana Hidalgo Editora, the house that has done the most to champion Di Benedetto's work since his death, did the same in 2017, under a similar title, *Trilogía: Las novelas de la espera* (Trilogy: The Novels of Expectation), drawn from the epigraph of *Zama*: "To the victims of expectation."

Saer's bold assertion that these books constitute a trilogy has thrived because reading them as a trilogy enriches each one, creating a whole greater than the sum of its parts. While their narratives are widely separated in time, a forward temporal current runs through them, making the overall tripartite structure echo that of *Zama*, which is divided into three sections titled 1790, 1794, and 1799. *The Silentiary* is set a century and a half later, in the recent past of the early 1950s, fifteen years or so before it was written, while *The Suicides* completes the movement into the present, taking place during the late 1960s, contemporary to when it was written and published.

In all three novels, the narrator's father is dead (an absence barely mentioned in *Zama* but crucial in *The Suicides*), while his mother and wife and/or lovers are alive and needy. Though no character explicitly reappears, the emphasis *Zama* places on Don Diego's name, combined with the marked namelessness of the two subsequent narrators, suggests that the protagonists of all three may be the same being, a man in his thirties, acted upon, remade, by different environments, expectations, and historical circumstances. Yet the three characters are also dissimilar, particularly in their relationship to writing. Don Diego is a bureaucrat who has no use for literature. The silentiary is also a bureaucrat, a mid-level corporate manager, but he dreams, fruitlessly, of being a writer. And the narrator of *The Suicides* is a working writer like Di Benedetto, who earned his living as a journalist for most of his life. The namelessness of the two latter protagonists hints that they are not only contemporaries of their author but also stand-ins for him.

That hypothesis is bolstered by Di Benedetto's decision to situate both *The Silentiary* and *The Suicides* in a nameless city that much resembles his native Mendoza, the capital of a wine-growing region in the west of Argentina. *The Silentiary* alludes several times to Mendoza's characteristic acequias, deep irrigation ditches originally dug by the Huarpe, an agricultural people who first settled the area in the third century AD. The acequias were such a successful water management system that their use expanded after the Spanish conquest, even in urban areas, where very deep gutters continue to imperil heedless pedestrians to this day.

The most powerful force acting upon these three novels to make them converge into a whole is not autobiography but history, the uncanny way the three books reverberate through the future course of their author's life and Argentine history. Which, in retrospect, they seem to expect. The ineluctable movement into the present they trace can also be read as a movement toward totalitarianism, which, with the support and consent of Secretary of State Henry Kissinger, came to full power in Argentina following a military coup d'état on March 24, 1976. That same day, officers came to arrest Di Benedetto as he sat working at his desk at the Mendoza newspaper *Los Andes*; for the next sixteen months he was imprisoned and tortured. Di Benedetto was fortunate. He was released and went into exile. Thirty thousand others were disappeared during the Dirty War. (One of the methods used—drugging prisoners and dropping them into the ocean from airplanes or helicopters—has lately been celebrated on T-shirts proudly sported at political rallies in the United States.)

A line from the early pages of *The Silentiary*—"The unending noise compels us to think of it, rather than anything else"—captures the cacophonous obliteration of normal social interaction, normal information exchange, that accompanies the descent into fascism. In its final pages, though, the novel's narrator may finally have learned that silence, the imposition of silence, is also a weapon. It was an avowed weapon of the Argentine dictatorship, as the journalist Uki

Goñi, an expert on the crimes of the Dirty War, had occasion to observe:

> One day, in 1974, I found myself frozen in my steps on the broad 9 de Julio Avenue that divides Buenos Aires in half. In the middle of this avenue rises a tall white obelisk...and inscribed upon it in large blue letters on a plain white background was the slogan "Silence Is Health."...[T]he billboard schooled Argentines in the total censorship and suppression of free speech that the dictatorship would soon impose...ostensibly to caution motorists against excessive use of the horn.

Two years later, the same words, "Silence Is Health," appeared on a banner hanging in a corridor of the Navy Mechanics School (or ESMA), after the dictatorship had transformed it into a clandestine center for torture and extermination. It was there to mock the prisoners, or warn them not to scream when they were seared with electric cattle prods.

Zama is both the longest and the most celebrated of the trilogy's novels, and that was the case well before the release of the 2017 film based on it by the Argentine director Lucrecia Martel, itself a masterpiece. The only work in the trilogy to receive an award at the time of its publication, however, was *The Silentiary*, which won the Gran Premio de Novela from Argentina's Subsecretaria de Cultura de la Nación—an odd prize which, for all the grandiosity of its name, seems to have been awarded only on that one occasion.

The late Argentine novelist Ricardo Piglia recalls in *The*

Diaries of Emilio Renzi, his fictionalized memoir, that a work by Di Benedetto that he calls *El hacedor de silencio* (The Maker of Silence)—a variant title Di Benedetto chose for a later edition of *The Silentiary*—was, in 1967, a finalist for a more prestigious award, the Premio Primera Plana-Sudamericana, judged by a panel of luminaries that included Leopoldo Marechal, Augusto Roa Bastos, and Gabriel García Márquez. In the end, Di Benedetto's work was first runner-up, a fate that chimes in perfectly with *The Silentiary*'s leery view of the hierarchies of literary reputation—the picture in a magazine of "Poet No. 3," or the "Second-Best Novelist" who "once sat at this very table." Perhaps that's why Piglia substituted it in. In fact, the Premio Primera Plana was for an unpublished novel, and it was *Los Suicidas*, just prior to its publication, that came in second, in 1968.

The conversation about Di Benedetto's work that the memoir records between its protagonist and García Márquez, on the night they first meet, has a ring of truth about it and could easily have concerned either of the two latter novels in the trilogy. García Márquez confesses to having "gone back and forth a great deal" while judging the prize, and to ultimately giving second place to Di Benedetto because his novel was too brief, not a novel at all. Piglia's character protests, pointing out that by the same logic "*Pedro Páramo* or, if you'll allow me, *No One Writes to the Colonel*, wouldn't have been considered in a novel competition either." In the conversation that ensues, the two writers "distinguish between short forms, medium-length stories, and novels."

The page count of the two latter novels is low; in the Adriana Hidalgo edition of the trilogy, *The Silentiary* and *The Suicides* come in at about 125 pages each. Such brevity, and the plentiful blank space on those pages, is an aspect of Di Benedetto's writing and of his character, which Saer calls "discretion" or "aesthetic sobriety," and Jimena Néspolo, in *Ejercicios de Pudor*, an influential work that revitalized Di Benedetto's reputation, refers to as "*pudor*" (modesty or reticence). In English we might describe it as understatedness. Di Benedetto's sentences do not seek to wow readers with their verbal dexterity; *The Silentiary* openly mocks the futility of that game: "Odious odysseys of words, oh Dios!" Di Benedetto's style actively courts underestimation, inviting the reader to overlook what he's doing, or dismiss it as minor, secondary. His music does not try to interrupt the noises of the world.

The most powerful element of his prose is not its diction or rhythm but the vastness of what the skein of words across the page summons up to leave unsaid—a vastness that, in *The Silentiary* in particular, is underscored by the ellipses that riddle almost every page. (By contrast, there's only one ellipsis in all of *Zama*, following a mention of the protagonist's name: "Doctor Don Diego de Zama! . . .") Most of *The Silentiary*'s ellipses occur in dialogues, as what the characters have voiced gives way to what they leave unspoken. But those trios of small dots also make their way into the narrator's authorial voice, the whole novel haunted by what it leaves out, what it does not attempt to capture in words.

In its current form, even the novel's last sentence includes an ellipsis. The final line of the first edition of *El silenciero*, however, was simply "La noche sigue." ("The night flows on.") Period. In 1975, the year before the Dirty War began, Di Benedetto revised the second edition brought out by the Buenos Aires house Orión. The text that Adriana Hidalgo Editore reissued in 1999 and has kept in print since—the text on which this translation is based—reflects the changes he made then. He added the brief, epigraph-like initial line that sets the scene for the novel, and made several other significant additions as well. Most notably, as Jimena Néspolo puts it in *Ejercicios de Pudor*, her landmark 2004 book on Di Benedetto, he "extended the novel's philosophical reflections."

In a 1969 essay about *The Silentiary* and *The Suicides*, the Paraguayan novelist Augusto Roa Bastos, the author of the great dictator novel *Yo, El Supremo* (*I the Supreme*), wrote of the two novels' "stance of verbal austerity, of return to the apparent initial poverty of language," which, he surmised, amounts to an "obliteration of the literary." He was struck, in particular, by the suspended ending of *The Silentiary*, whose narrator reaches no conclusions but negates himself, "places himself in parentheses, relegates himself to the unnamable, which restores him to silence, as the only way of affirming the victory over noise."

In 1975, Di Benedetto added five new sentences to the final passage, where the protagonist, now in prison, has a dream. He did not know that he would soon be in prison himself, and that he would smuggle out the short stories he managed to write there—later published under the title *Absurdos*—by including them in his letters as descriptions of dreams. He did not know how soon history would rush into his novel's silent ellipses, filling them with new meanings of its own and transforming its inconclusive ending into one of chilling prescience.

According to his friends, Di Benedetto rarely spoke of the terrible months he spent in the dungeons of fascist Argentina. Perhaps he was unwilling to be defined by the worst thing the world imposed on him, or perhaps, like Besarión, he was superstitious: "When the things we fear move away from us, they'll return if we name them. They'll mistake the mention of their name for a call to come back." The 1975 changes to the ending of *The Silentiary* can be read as a statement about the nightmare to come, all the stronger for having been made before it came. The new lines summarily reject any possibility of "victory over noise," any hope the original text might have held out for some redemptive or expiatory meaning to its narrator's suffering. Instead, they relegate that suffering even further into the realm of the unsayable.

> The sudden return of the shepherd comes as a surprise. He reproaches me. "Don't pretend you've been given in sacrifice, or immolated!"
> I'm about to reject his presumption (glimpsing, nevertheless, the truth that it reveals). I try to reproach him for his haughtiness, his indifference to my humility... But I stammer and can't manage to get it out.

What the future held in store was still in the future when Di Benedetto added, to the novel's final "The night flows on," an ellipsis and a new final phrase "...y no es hacia la paz adonde fluye" "...and not toward peace."

—ESTHER ALLEN